Read My Lips

Jana Novotny Hunter was born in Czechoslovakia and grew up in England in what she calls a "noisy continental home". Two of her siblings were born profoundly deaf, and Jana says this served as the inspiration for writing *Read My Lips*. "Growing up with a deaf brother and sister who chose opposite methods of communication (and continue to have problems with each other as a result), I have long been fascinated by issues relating to communication. This has been underscored by the language differences I experienced myself as part of a Czech family living in England." A graduate of Hornsey College of Art, Jana married an American and spent many years living in California, where she worked as a textile designer, teacher, writer and mum. She now lives   mily in a tiny village in Rutland, working as a   iting lecturer at universities and colleges, a sp   schools, libraries and at conferences, and ar   or for children's books and television.

Read My Lips

Jana Novotny Hunter

WALKER BOOKS
AND SUBSIDIARIES
LONDON • BOSTON • SYDNEY

First published 2002 by Walker Books Ltd
87 Vauxhall Walk, London SE11 5HJ

2 4 6 8 10 9 7 5 3 1

Text © 2002 Jana Novotny Hunter
Cover image: Bruce Laurance/Getty Images
Cover design by Walker Books Ltd

This book has been typeset in Frutiger

Printed in Great Britain by Cox & Wyman Ltd, Reading, Berkshire

British Library Cataloguing in Publication Data:
a catalogue record for this book is
available from the British Library

ISBN 0-7445-9053-1

For Debbie and Stephen,
my sister and brother, who had
the courage to choose

With grateful thanks to Judy Blume and the
Society of Children's Book Writers and
Illustrators for the Works-in-Progress prize.
Also heartfelt thanks to the students and staff
of Riverside School for the Hearing Impaired,
Greater Los Angeles Association for the Deaf,
Clodagh Corcoran, Richard Hunter and,
of course, the real "Cat".

Prologue

My head bursts.

"Mummy. I want my mummy. Mummy, come and get me..." Tears burn my cheeks as hands pull on my pyjamas. A white-coated nurse, her head a tiny pink bead, drifts high above me, very far off. She's smaller than a pinprick but her hands are so big they can reach me way, way up here on my floating, faraway bed...

"Noooo! No more hurt! Mummy! Come and get me!"

I pound on the nurse's white front. But my small fists can't stop her and her needle pricks my bottom.

Hurt. Bottom hurts.

Head hurts.

Ears hurt.

Hurt, hurt, HURT.

Mummy, make the hurt go away.

"Mummy!" I open my mouth and scream.

But no sound comes out.

I scream and scream, but there is only silence.

Mummy has left me alone in the silence...

SILENCE.

Chapter One

I was five years old when I went deaf.

Up until then I heard everything. Voices, the cat purring, the sound of Mum's slippers on the stairs – even my own voice talking breathlessly on the phone...

"Daddy, Daddy! I can spell my own name! It's D-E-B-B-I-E."

"You *are* Daddy's clever girl!"

It was as if all the tinkling, whirring, booming, banging, happy noises of my world sounded just for me, until suddenly a gigantic explosion of pain went off in my head, and *poof!* SILENCE.

I've not spoken since.

Traumatized, I simply retreated into a void of silence. I didn't understand. How could any little kid understand that she'd caught meningitis and lost her hearing for ever? Or that her parents were just as scared and confused as she was? All I knew was I was very, very frightened and very, very alone in a strange, new and silent world.

And that's when they sent me away.

They sent me to the Residential School for the Hearing Impaired (nicknamed deaf city by us kids). And if getting meningitis and going deaf was painful, terrible, scary and a whole lot more, being sent away was even worse.

It felt like a giant punishment for getting sick.

As if my parents loved me when I was healthy and had two ears that worked, but the moment I stopped talking and hearing they couldn't wait to get rid of me. If it hadn't been for my best friend, Bee James, I probably would've gone mad as well as deaf.

Bee's been my best friend ever since those first nightmare days when I spent all my time hiding under my bed, sucking the tail of my toy cat, Fluffy. Everyone and everything beyond that bed was a horror to me – the kids using sign language, the teachers mouthing silent words... It was like a creepy ghost-train ride at a fairground.

Bee understood that.

Bee understood and she kept my hiding place a secret. But, every now and then, she'd poke her toffee-coloured head under the bed, point at Fluffy and make funny faces at me. At first I thought she wanted Fluffy for herself, and I clung onto his lumpy body harder than ever. But then I saw that this pixie-faced kid actually wanted to show me something. Over and over again Bee pointed to Fluffy and made a sign of two fingers stroking imaginary whiskers.

It took me a while to make the connection, but when I did it was like a giant light bulb going on in my head. That sign and the toy were the same thing!

The stroking whiskers sign that Bee was making meant cat just like the sound you made with your voice meant cat! Just like the letters C-A-T spelled out in my alphabet book meant cat.

In a rush of excitement I crawled out from under the bed and made the sign myself.

"CAT!"

"Cat, cat, cat!"

Bee nodded delightedly and we laughed and threw the long-suffering Fluffy into the air for joy.

And that's when Cat became my sign name, my shorthand nickname in sign language.

It's been twelve years since I, Debbie Katz, became Cat, and it took at least two of those years to stop hating it here and grow to love it. Now I love the secret hideaway feel of deaf city with its woody smells and red brick buildings nestling in a valley below the hills. Rumour has it they built the place in the hills to keep us in, but I think it was to keep the rest of the world out.

If you want to know what I'm like – well, I'm like any other teenage girl I suppose, dreaming one minute about my future as a hotshot lawyer and the next minute about boys. I can be giggly and immature, then grown up and serious in the space of seconds, and like any other kid I get sick of working my socks off at school. The only difference between me and most other teenagers is that I communicate in sign language.

Looks-wise, I'm sometimes pretty (sometimes definitely not) with a tangle of curly dark red hair. I'm kind of tall and lanky, which does have its advantages – my one claim to fame is that I hold the school cup for cross-country. I have a smiley face for the world and a secret knot of worries in the pit of my stomach about life on the outside in the big scary world of the hearing. Because, terrifying as it was coming here, the thought of leaving it now is even worse...

I try to discuss this with Bee today.

We're sitting in the stands, in the late September sun, waiting for a football match to start, and Bee's reminding me yet again how I must find someone to take me to the Christmas ball. (A big anxiety which drips onto the murky waters of my even bigger fear – that of going on the outside.)

"Bee, don't you ever feel nervous?" I say. "You know, about leaving here at the end of the year?"

"Leaving school isn't something we can avoid," answers Bee practically. "Going to the ball on your own is." To Bee not having a boyfriend is a serious condition, comparable with the loss of a limb.

I sigh. "Finding a boyfriend is all part of the same problem, Bee. You know, the problem of being cocooned in our own world up here. The boys here feel so much like family, it'd be like going out with my own brother."

This is true. We've been in this secluded school so long, it's like we're all welded together at the hip. And it's pretty hard to get romantic with someone you've known since the snotty-nose and bogeys stage.

"Maybe you should try hypnosis," suggests Bee. "It's supposed to work with phobias."

"Thanks a lot!" In an effort to cure myself of my ghastly affliction, I gaze hopefully at the spindly form of Dave Grant loping onto the pitch. But I'm just not interested.

"It's hopeless, Bee."

Bee's just about to launch into another attack on my pickiness, when a couple of speaker kids wander over to our section of the stands. They are having to concentrate so hard on lip-reading each other, they're oblivious to the fact they're breaking deaf city's unwritten rule...

Speakers and signers don't mix.

"They'll get lynched!" Bee rattles the stands until the kids feel the vibrations and look up. "Get over the other side quick," she motions. "This is the signers' area."

The kids jump up like scalded cats and leg it over to the other side. Deaf city is divided into speakers and signers, and the two groups are sworn enemies. Even today's football match, supposed

16

to be upper sixth against lower sixth, is really between the two warring groups.

Signers, like me and Bee, think speakers cop out of being deaf by trying to act like hearing people and speakers think signers make the deaf look weird with their signs. It's an issue that divides the whole deaf community, not just our school, but still our head-teacher, Mr Kaplan, keeps trying to get us to mix. Kaplan's very big on total communication, a combination of speech and sign that blends the two methods. He thinks that if everyone used total communication there wouldn't be this split. As if!

I used to believe the deaf city war being played out here was the way it had to be. But lately I've been wondering. Why should we have to take sides? And secretly, very secretly, a growing part of me wants to know...

What's it like to be a speaker?

Chapter Two

The football match kicks off, and for a while I forget all about the deaf city war. Sport is a complete escape for me – it's so great to let your mind go and concentrate on physical stuff. With my long legs, running fast is a given, so I'm never happier than when I'm out there racing and winning cups.

On the pitch the match is going OK, until our team gets a corner. Jack Boldwood, the boy from our deaf culture class who's going out with Bee, is about to position the ball, when, without warning, he hurls it to the ground and makes the angry sign of "Foul! Foul!"

"What's happened?" asks Bee.

I squint in the sun so I can read Jack's signs.

"He says some of the speakers on the other team have been lip-reading to get an unfair advantage."

It *is* an unfair advantage. When you communicate in sign, everyone at deaf city, including the opposing team, can see it, but if you use your voice, only those who lip-read can get it. That's why the rule at deaf city is that everybody sticks to basic sign symbols for sport. If the speakers use their voices during a match, it gives them the edge.

"Stick to symbols, speaker!" demands Jack. "Work out a code like the rest of us!"

"Just like a signer to cop out of losing!"

"Just like a speaker to cop out of being deaf!"

"Rotten speaker!"

"*Idiot* signer!"

Someone hits out. It's Max Manus, the most muscly bloke in our year.

The referee orders Max off the pitch, but he just stands there snorting steam like a belligerent bull. Mr Kaplan arrives on the scene, waving his arms about. Even huge guys with muscles for brains obey deaf city's little barrel of a head-teacher.

But not today.

Today it takes Kaplan, two other teachers and a giant threat of suspension before things calm down. Nobody wants to be sent home right at the start of term.

"OK, everyone. Let's get back to the match," commands the referee, and reluctantly the two teams get back into position. But their body language is no longer easy and sportsmanlike; it's reined in, taut with aggression. As if someone's put a giant lid on a pot that's still boiling.

I can remember just how that feels...

Like a time traveller, I'm back in those early deaf city days. There I was, this little kid who'd had a break-through in sign language, quite happy to learn all the different signs and communicate with the other kids. Bee was my friend and I was content because, peaceful in a silent world of movement and colours, I was waiting...

Waiting for my hearing to come back.

I actually imagined my hearing would come back as easily as good health after a bout of chicken-pox! I thought my ears would get better like the time I had an ear infection and had to take medicine four times a day. How could I have been so naive?

But as days turned into weeks, I gave up hoping it would happen soon. At deaf city I thought only *kids* were deaf, and that it was one of those things you grew out of like small feet and scabby knees. Hearing was for grown-ups – parents and doctors. That meant my hearing would come back when I grew up.

Then one day we got a new teacher.

Her name was Miss Ball. She had shoulder-length floppy hair and pointy tortoiseshell glasses. I was so fascinated by those glasses, I didn't notice anything else about Miss Ball at first. I watched her glasses flash as she talked to us in sign language, and adored her.

We were all sitting cross-legged on the story rug while Miss Ball showed us pictures of kids to explain different emotions. One kid was happy, another sad, another anxious... When Miss Ball came to the angry kid, she pointed to me with a questioning look. Pleased to be picked by the new teacher, I was just about to answer, when something happened.

Miss Ball tilted her head in a questioning way, and as she did so a section of her shiny, floppy hair slid away to reveal a secret. A nasty, horrible secret.

Miss Ball was wearing a hearing aid!

Rigid with shock, I stared. Why was she wearing that?

21

Unaware of my horror, Miss Ball pointed again to the angry picture and screwed up her own face, mimicking the emotion to give me a clue to the answer. Surely I could identify this feeling, she seemed to say.

Huh!

Not only could I name it, I *felt* it! Rage, terrible rage, welled up inside me. Rage that I'd kept down since going deaf. Bubbling rage I'd controlled for months and months with a stony-faced silence. Now, in defiant, cathartic fury, I let those feelings go. I opened my mouth and gave one almighty scream.

"Aaaagghh!"

The kids stared.

"Aaaagghh! Aaaagghh!"

Miss Ball waited calmly.

"Aaaagghh! Aaaagghh! Aaaagghh!" I screamed over and over again.

When I hadn't a puff of breath left in me to scream any more, Miss Ball moved in gentle response. "Please use only sign language in this class," she asked sweetly, "because I am deaf too." She pointed to the small flesh-coloured aids nestling in her ears.

A sense of amazement shot through the room. The kids laughed and gestured in happy surprise. At last someone was like them! They were all thrilled to bits.

All except me.

I'd been duped. Tricked like Red Riding Hood when she discovered her sweet granny was really a wolf. I *hated* Miss Ball and her stupid tortoiseshell glasses! Hated her patient, gentle signing. But most of all I hated her sly, stowaway aids.

I wanted to smash them!

Smash them and crush them into thousands of little pieces. Because that's when I knew the terrible truth.

You stayed like this for ever...

Chapter Three

The football match is a walkover. Two–nil to the upper sixth. Our team hangs around the pitch to thrash out the result, but Bee and I are both feeling too jangled up to join in, so we head for the senior common room to get a Coke.

Despondently Bee flops onto the wide window ledge of the common room to stare out of the window.

"Signers should teach those cheating speakers a lesson," she says.

Making a face, I quote Mr Kaplan's favourite phrase. "'But at our school, we're one big happy family. Speakers are our *brothers*, our sisters.'"

At that Bee waggles her tongue at me in mimicry of our speaker sisters. I'm just about to swat her when Apeman barges into the comm

Officially known as Mr Davis, Ape

biggest slave-driver in the social studies dep

ment. Some say he got his nickname from his

favourite expression – "It's a jungle out there" –

but others reckon it's because he resembles an

escapee from *Planet of the Apes*. Apeman became

hard of hearing when he was twenty, and he main-

tains that the only reason he's so strict with us

is because he knows *personally* how hard it is in

the real world.

What an excuse. Some people are just born

mean. It's typical the way Apeman storms in, pins

a flyer onto the noticeboard and bulldozes out of

the room without so much as a nod at us lowly

students.

"Come and visit any time, Apeman," Bee signs

to his retreating back.

"Don't forget to knock first." Even if he used

a sledgehammer, we wouldn't hear.

"Wonder what new torture he has in mind?"

"Probably some research programme on how

much misery teenagers can stand." I saunter over

to the noticeboard. "He certainly—" But when

I see the flyer Apeman's tacked up, I gasp. "Bee,

...peman's opened the Outsiders to
...ers!"

...so?"

"So I've been wanting to get into that club for ages. It'd be great to go out in a group and visit places."

"You know only speakers get into that club." Bee explains to me very patiently, as if she's talking to a child. "Speakers can use their voices, Cat. If they get into trouble, they can communicate with anyone."

"I want to join that club."

Bee clasps her hands in mock reverence. "And mingle with *real people* on the outside?"

Bee's sarcasm stings. In year seven we vowed not to deal with the outside. We felt that our life was with the deaf and we were gonna stick with them. The hearing world didn't understand us and we didn't understand them so there was no point trying to mix. We've always been together in this before. Am I turning my back on our vow?

But suddenly the thought that's been churning inside me for weeks has to burst free. "Bee, we must find a way to make it on the outside sometime! We won't be cocooned in deaf city for much longer."

"So?" Bee picks up a pack of cards lying on the bookshelf and starts to shuffle them dismissively.

"I'm going to see Apeman before school tomorrow and ask if he'll take me."

Bee slams the pack of cards onto the table and glares at me.

"Bee, don't you realize it was OK to stay inside deaf city's walls when we were kids, but when we leave we'll be on our own? Alone in the silence without any support from our friends, or deaf city..." A repeat performance of the terror I felt at five years old is more than I can bear.

"People only laugh if you use your voice," Bee signs to me angrily. "I'll never be a speaker."

"But—"

Bee's face is really angry now. "Don't you get it, Cat? Or have you forgotten? Deafies who try to speak are traitors. They're token deafies in a hearing world, because they turn their backs on the true deaf way of communicating. Speakers are the enemy."

In bed that night I think about the enemy.

Will I become one of them if I join the Outsiders? Will I be putting myself in the firing line just like

27

those gang members who drive through enemy territory and end up getting shot?

It's too scary even to think about.

Maybe I should let my desire to join a speakers' club stay buried deep inside me like the voice I once had. Leave it as a dream. Because that's all I can do these days. Dream, dream, dream. Even now as I drift off to sleep, I'm dreaming my favourite dream. The dream of the disappearing boy...

It was the day before the summer holidays, and the disappearing boy was waiting outside Kaplan's office – all six foot of him. He was a stranger to deaf city and I couldn't help staring at his curly brown hair and tanned arms. Naturally he noticed me gaping at him like some star-struck fish, and in the split second before I clamped my gawping mouth shut, he caught my eye. He caught my eye and smiled a gorgeous, dimpled smile and ... I practically passed out! But before I could make any more of an idiot of myself, the school secretary bustled out and hustled the stranger into the office. And that was it. I never saw him again.

So the sum total of my boy experience is a *non-event*!

I wake up next morning to the vibrations of my

silent alarm clock. The way things are going, it'll probably be the most exciting thing ever to happen in any bed of mine!

Today I'm going to see Apeman about the Outsiders.

I am so nervous.

At the door to Apeman's classroom, I stall. What am I doing risking everything – my best friend and our vow to have a comfortable life with our own kind? It's madness. Turning away in defeat, I'm so distracted I bump into Myra Ryder and her two hangers-on, Jude Wyatt and Sherry Tate, the most unpopular signers at deaf city. They always love a chance to whip up discord in school, and today is no exception.

"Those pathetic speakers think they can suck up to hearies by talking," Myra is signing sulkily. "They're traitors to their own kind."

"You said it." Sherry and Jude are sucking up to their leader as usual.

A stubborn flame flares up inside me. This lot would like to poison the whole of deaf city with their suspicion and hatred. Well, they won't poison me. With renewed determination I march back to Apeman's door and press the light buzzer.

29

In a gush of air the door is flung open, sucking out the air in my lungs at the same time. Because there, standing next to Apeman's desk and holding the Outsiders' signing-up sheet, is a boy with "gorgeous" tattooed over every inch of his six-foot body.

The disappearing boy!

And I can see from the way he's talking to Apeman that the boy of my dreams is a speaker.

Chapter Four

Apeman speaks and signs at the same time. "What is it, Cat?"

"Um..." I stare up at the familiar posters of history heroes on his wall – Scott of the Antarctic, Nelson and Walter Raleigh. They all seem to be watching me, expecting me to be equally courageous. "Um ... the Outsiders?"

"Yes?"

"Um..." Why do boys you like only disappear when you don't want them to? When you wish they'd vanish, they stand about looking utterly gorgeous. "I ... I've come to sign up for the Outsiders."

"The Outsiders is an oral club." As if I didn't know. "So, how are your speech-reading grades?"

"Fine, Mr Davis." Liar!

"Then how come you're not using your voice right now?"

Trust Apeman.

If only I could shout, "I don't use my voice any more because it went the same place as my hearing: DOWN THE TUBES!" But I can't. I just stand there like a fool, staring at the stapler on Apeman's desk.

Then out of the corner of my eye I see the signing-up sheet edging towards me. I follow the trail from the sheet, along a tanned arm, to a dimpled smile that could make a pet rock speak. The disappearing boy is encouraging me to sign up! With shaking fingers, I take the pen he offers me and, acting like I'm used to the world dissolving under my legs, I sign my name:

Debbie Katz

right next to his:

Joey Estrada

So that our signatures *actually touch*.

But before I have a chance to pass out with joy,

Apeman grabs the paper with his big, insensitive paw. "OK, Cat. I'll check with Miss Alexander on your speech-reading grades. I'm sure you realize why the Outsiders requires its members to speak."

"Yes, yes. I do. Well. Thank you, Mr Davis. Thank you, sir..." Nodding and smiling like an idiot, I make the kind of exit no girl trying to look winsome and alluring should ever make.

Well! If I wanted to join that club before, now it's a matter of love life and death!

Joey Estrada, who I've not bumped into since that day in the summer when he enrolled, is in the club! Dimpled, brown-eyed Joey Estrada, the boy of my dreams... Running down the empty hall, I realize I'm trembling like a jelly. A jelly brought back to earth with a massive splat when I realize first period, deaf culture, has already started.

Miss Alexander – Aggy – may be my favourite teacher at deaf city, but she's also a stickler for punctuality. "Sorry, Aggy," I apologize. "I don't have a late pass. I was with Mr Davis."

Miss Alexander takes the class register and puts an L next to my name. She's wearing one of her multicoloured outfits today, but she means business.

"Sit down, Cat. We're discussing topics for the debate."

My classmates are already seated in a discussion circle, and even the rearranged desks have an air of expectation.

"What happened?" Bee whispers as I slide into the seat next to her.

I roll my eyes. "I just met my date for the ball."

Bee's jaw drops. *"Apeman?!"*

Before I have a chance to explain, Aggy orders, "No more interruptions, Cat. The debate will be here before we know it."

The debate. That's when students from the upper sixth debate in front of the whole school, and it's the signal for all the end-of-term stuff to start.

"Suggestions for topics?" Aggy, like all teachers at deaf city, uses total communication, though her voice is wasted on most of us. Today, I realize, I'm beginning to see Kaplan's pet project – total communication with the teachers – in a new light. "Remember that the topic must be framed as a statement," Aggy reminds us.

Megan Gerard, a girl from our dorm who uses natural henna for her hair and green polish for her fingernails in recognition of Greenpeace, is signing something. "I think nuclear waste is an important issue," she suggests.

Jack Boldwood, the man who's always ready with an argument, interrupts. "I know nuclear waste's important, but we've already done it in social studies."

"How about human waste?" someone jokes, and everybody starts laughing. "Plenty of it around here."

Aggy shakes her head. "Cat, maybe you have a better suggestion?"

"Er, not really..." How can I concentrate on debate topics when I'm fantasizing about Joey and worrying about my speech-reading grades?

"Cat!" Aggy is taken aback. "A girl who plans to go into law needs all the practice she can get at debating. Surely there's *something* you feel strongly about?"

Aggy's right, of course. There *is* something I feel very strongly about, but it's off-limits. The forbidden subject that divides deaf city, and that's throbbing inside my brain like a drum.

"Oral. Manual," I finally let out.

"Yes?"

"We should discuss oral communication versus manual. Speakers versus signers."

There is a ripple of excitement. Even Myra Ryder stops chewing on her snaggly nails and glares at me.

"That's a very *personal* issue, Cat."

"That's why we should do it! This ... this deaf city war has been going on too long!" My heart beats faster as I see nods of agreement. "It's time signers and speakers learned to get on with one another."

"What a dreamer!" Jack's crew cut seems to bristle with disgust. "Speakers and signers will never unite."

"I still think we should try."

Aggy nods. "Cat, your ideals are good. But it's a little romantic to think—"

"What's wrong with romance?" quips Bee in an effort to change the subject. "I think we should discuss why boys—"

But Aggy cuts in. "The oral/manual topic's too touchy. You'd have the student body fighting, the teachers at loggerheads..."

"But, Aggy, we have that already," Lyn Leonard points out. "Look at the fight at the match yesterday."

"Lyn's right," agrees Lyn's best friend, Stephanie Bell, shaking her ponytail. "Things couldn't be any worse."

Suddenly hands everywhere fly about.

"Let's show those speakers!"

"Signers for ever!"

"Speakers rule!"

I have really stirred them up.

Aggy lets us have our say. She's never forgotten how it felt to have her hands tied down as a child because she wasn't supposed to use sign, so in her class she encourages us to air our feelings.

But when opinions threaten to overheat, Aggy motions us to stop. "OK, OK. Calm down, calm down, everyone."

There's a moment's stillness while Aggy waits for us to settle, then she drops her bombshell. "Well ... it might be opening Pandora's box, but..."

"You'll let the demons out!" finishes Jack, waggling his fingers like a pair of devil's horns.

"Well ... I've never seen this class so motivated."

The room vibrates with feet-stomping and clapping.

"I have the motion." Jumping up, I rush to the chalkboard and scrawl across it:

*The deaf should fit in
with the hearing world.*

There are boos and cheers. A spitball zooms past my ear and splats against the board.

There are furious nods of agreement as Aggy signs, "That is a very emotive statement!"

Fortunately Aggy misses the "statement" Myra Ryder makes to me at that moment. It's just one sign, but you don't have to understand sign language to know what she means!

Jack waves his arm. "I want to speak against the motion! Show those speakers who's stupid. Signers are the only deafies true to themselves." Jack's parents are both fighters for deaf rights. The whole family, including his ancient cocker spaniel, are totally deaf.

"Hold it for a minute, Jack." Aggy looks straight at me. "We'll have that motion on one condition. The speaker *for* the motion will be you, Cat."

"But ... just because I made the motion, it doesn't mean..."

"The point of a debate is that you must be able to put forward your case logically, whatever you believe personally. It will be good experience, Cat."

38

"But..." What would Aggy think about my plan to join an oral club too?

"Think about it."

I try to catch Bee's eye, but she turns her head to avoid my gaze. She nods with Jack conspiratorially, then, defiant and hostile, the pair of them raise their arms in the deaf power salute.

Oh, Bee. I'm not against you.

That gesture symbolizes the right of the deaf not to struggle to fit in with a world where the hearing rule. It's a symbol of solidarity and strength, but right now it saps the enthusiasm out of me.

Myra-the-Spider Ryder, not missing an opportunity to gang up against me, raises her skinny arm too. "Deaf power!"

Cheers, taunts and jeers whirr around me. *Should* the deaf fit in? I've never thought so before, but lately I don't know. If this feud is never brought out into the open it will go on forever boiling, bubbling beneath the surface.

Like my voice when I was five years old.

Needing space, I close my eyes to the signing. Admit it, Cat, you love a challenge. A part of you feeds on being a leader, a fighter for causes. Why else would you want to study law? It was you who got the lower sixth kitchen privileges; you and Bee who organized the dining-hall riots...

"I'll do it!"

Aggy nods. "Good."

More cheers and desk pounding.

"Go for it, Cat!"

Mercifully the light flashes then, signalling the end of first period, and I'm swamped by a crowd of students thumping me on the back, congratulating me, telling me what to say.

No going back now.

But when I catch sight of Bee hastily stuffing books into her bag, I almost wish I could. "Bee? Bee, wait!"

Aloof and cold, Bee flicks back her long toffee-coloured hair. "I'm off to the play auditions," she retorts, and she stalks out the room, dragging Jack with her.

Myra bars my way. "You should be speaking *against* the motion, not *for* it," she sneers. "Or have you already gone over to the other side?"

"What d'you mean?"

She turns her insect body and scowls at me. "You know what I mean, *speaker*!"

Myra's jealousy of my running ability has bugged

her since I broke her cross-country record in year eight. So now she's found the perfect excuse to be my enemy in public!

The worst part is, I wonder if there's some truth in her taunt. *Am* I going over to the other side?

Chapter Five

Myra Ryder is not going to scare me off.

Before I write my speech, I'll poll deaf city and get to the truth about how kids around here feel. That way I'll be the "voice" of deaf city and ignoring vicious personal attacks like Myra's will be easier.

Of course, I could really do a good job if I sat in on some speech-reading classes...

It wouldn't be spying; it'd be research. And it might have the added bonus of helping me get into the Outsiders with Joey Estrada.

Who am I kidding?

I want to learn to speak again, and like Myra I've just found a good excuse to do what deep down I've wanted to do for a very long time.

Resolved to do whatever it takes, I slam the classroom door behind me.

Outside in the corridor, lockers fly open and the whole second floor vibrates as a thick stream of bodies moves past. In the middle of the throng Kaplan's having a go at Rob Walker, a speaker who I know from track meetings, about not wearing his hearing aid. Poor old Rob's trying to explain that his aid picks up too much static, but Kaplan's not paying any attention.

"Rob, you must wear your aid to benefit from what hearing you have."

I interrupt with a wave of my hand, and despite Rob's allegiance to the speaker side he flashes me a grateful look.

But Kaplan still goes on with his usual lecture. "We believe total communication is the best way for you to communicate. With total communication you'll be able to talk with everybody no matter what your level of hearing."

If Kaplan had his way the whole world, deaf *and* hearing, would use total communication!

"Excuse me, Mr Kaplan." I try again. "I need to discuss my timetable with you."

Kaplan frowns. "What is it, Cat?"

"Um ... Mr Kaplan, I want ... I *need* to get back into the speech-reading programme."

Kaplan's bottle-brush eyebrows shoot up. "But I seem to remember you refused to participate last year."

"I want to try again. Please, Mr Kaplan. I'll work really, really hard."

"Hmm." I can see him thinking, Goody, goody, another convert to total communication! "Well, I need to look up your files. Your audiograms..."

My heart sinks. Audiograms register hearing loss and mine show I'm profoundly deaf.

"I *was* hearing until I was five, sir."

"Yes, I remember, Cat," says Kaplan, pointedly using his voice as he signs. "I'll see what I can do. Get to your class, now; the light's already flashed. You too, Rob, and don't let me see you without your aid again."

"Thank you, Mr Kaplan, thank you!"

I practically dance to second period. *I'm going to learn to speak again! To speak, speak, speak!* But then I stop myself guiltily. What am I getting so excited about?

I'm a signer.

The rest of the morning I'm on a knife-edge,

balanced between elation and fear. The way my heart is crashing under my ribs, either one could kill me.

At lunchtime I dash to the dining-hall in the hope of finding Bee and telling her about Joey. That's one development my romantic room-mate *will* approve of!

In the dining-hall the familiar smell of hamburger and warm carrots hits me. Nervously I scan the tables for Bee's long toffee-coloured hair but she's not there, although I can see someone waving to me from the queue.

"Hi, Cat!"

"Hi."

It's Rob Walker. "Great motion for the debate!" Rob signs to me, braving looks from kids astounded to see a speaker talking to a signer.

"Thanks." I acknowledge Rob's return of my favour to him earlier. "I think so too."

A group of speakers, seeing his gesture, point at me and stare (news travels fast at deaf city), and their reaction spreads to the next table. Ignoring them, I pick up a tray and join the queue. But there's no escape, because even the pimply guy serving makes a disgusting sign with a hot dog.

People with that kind of humour shouldn't be around food in my opinion.

"Pay no attention to him," advises spiky-haired Megan Gerard, who's in front of me in the queue. "*I* think you're brave to speak for the motion, especially since you don't believe it."

Gulp.

"Want any help?"

"Thanks, but Bee has already agreed to poll the school with me." I'm getting good at telling lies these days.

Later, on my way to the dorm, I'm praying Bee will turn my lie to Megan into the truth. I've not seen my best friend all afternoon and that's proof she's still angry with me. When I get there she is spread glamorously across her bed, like some Hollywood actress, reading a script.

"Is that the school play? Did you get the part you wanted?"

Bee nods frostily. I know every one of Bee's moods, especially this one. OK, Miss Ice Queen, don't bubble over about the play and the part you've got in it! Stick to your mood like glue if you want because I, Debbie Katz, happen to be an expert in mood alteration.

46

Secure in the knowledge that ice queens must keep their eyes glued to their script rather than bestow a look on their lowly friends, I slide out the vibrating alarm from under my mattress. Then I slip it under Bee's duvet and flip the switch.

Suddenly the whole bed trembles. Bee drops her script as vibrations travel up her legs and begin to shake her. She tries to keep a straight face, but as her body starts to wobble she can't help giggling. "Debbie Katz, you're a..." Jiggling and giggling, Bee throws the script at me and the tension dissolves.

Now's the time to tell Bee about my idea of polling deaf city. "Please, Bee. Will you help me make up a questionnaire? I really want to get the true feelings of everyone for the debate, so I can be their spokesperson."

"Well, you've already got *my* feelings!"

"But you're just one person. And see how wound up you are! This really matters to all of us."

No response.

"Help me poll the school," I plead. "You know, find out how students feel about whether deaf and hearing kids should go out with each other, get married, have *sex*..."

"Have sex?" The question piques Bee's interest despite herself.

"That's right," I say. "I've already told Megan you're my research assistant. She wanted to help me and ... but I'd rather you... Oh, please don't make me a liar, Bee. You're my best friend..."

"You told Megan I was your *research assistant*?" Bee's love of drama makes her overreact sometimes.

"It happened before I knew it."

"Doesn't what *I* want matter here?"

"Of course it does. You're playing the part of the flirt in the play," I say slyly. "And you're going to need a lot of help learning your lines."

"What are you getting at?"

"Well, you know. You'll need a best friend, the one who *always* helps you out." I give Bee an affectionate hug and she grins up at me. "Someone who's worked on scripts with you before..."

"I get to ask the boys in our year intimate questions, right?" is Bee's question.

"You can ask them anything. What they like to eat, to drink, to *kiss*..."

Bee laughs.

"I knew that last question would win you over!"

48

"Too right! You know I'm only doing it because you're my best friend. Really I hate the whole idea... OK, who shall we ask first?"

"Bee, there's only one person I want to quiz..." I am bursting to tell her about Joey Estrada and his rescue of me. "Because... Oh, Bee, I think I'm falling in love with a speaker."

Chapter Six

But for days I don't even *see* Joey.

My dreams of him are like my dreams of becoming a speaker. Doomed.

I'm the last in our whole dorm to have a boyfriend. I know this because nothing's private around here. Our dorm is made up of four partitioned units (each shared by two girls) of dog-kennel proportions with dividing walls which stop a foot from the ceiling. I suppose the architect realized noise wouldn't be a problem with hard-of-hearing kids, but what about privacy? In our dorm, when somebody wants to tell secrets to her friend next door, she writes words on the ceiling with a torch and everybody can read them. It's galling to know I've no secrets to tell.

Our unit looks like a battle zone tonight. Bee and I are working on the questionnaire together and balls of paper, empty cups and apple cores litter the floor. A pile of dirty laundry has spilled off the chair, mixed with the clean clothes I keep meaning to put away, and a stack of books has tumbled into it. Luckily Aggy's in charge of our dorm, and she's pretty cool about mess at weekends. She says as long as she never has to come face to face with a rat we can live in our own squalor till Monday.

"Hey, Bee, how about a question on the police, something like 'Should the police learn sign language?' Remember that man who was shot when he went to sign because the police thought he was reaching for a gun?"

"Yeah, but I can't think any more." Bee leans back on her haunches and groans. "I'm too hungry."

"I do remember something in the dim and distant past called food..."

Bee throws a crumpled piece of paper at me. "All the good stuff will be gone if you don't get a move on."

"Wait a second." I run over to the mirror, slick on some lip gloss and run my fingers through my bushy red hair. You never know who might be in the dining-hall.

Bee points a shaky finger at my glistening lips. "I smell fruit. Is that stuff edible?"

"Not unless you're constipated. It's called Passionate Prune." And on that inspiring note we make our giggling way to the dining-hall.

Dinner's almost over when we get there. The long trestle-tables have been cleared and it looks like there are only leftovers and bottles of ketchup remaining. Deaf city food used to be terrible but it improved overnight when Bee and I organized the dining-hall riots. (Though you'd never know it from the shrivelled burgers and dead-eye eggs left to tempt us tonight.)

"Look at this pigswill," I complain, staring in disgust at a congealed tray of stew.

Bee slops some onto a plate and squashes her nose like a pig's snout. "Oink, oink."

I grab a lukewarm hamburger and scan the tables for Joey. I've tried coming early, staying a long time and now coming late, but he's never here. Doesn't the boy eat?!

Stephanie and Lyn, nicknamed the deaf city twins because they dress and act alike, notice us and come over to our table, their identical ponytails bouncing in time together. (It's rumoured those two do everything together, but that can't be true. Lyn's going out with Max, and he's certainly not known for his gentle sharing qualities.)

"We've been talking about the debate," announces Stephanie, perching her backside right next to my unappetizing plate of food.

"Yeah, and we think you should pull out!"

Carefully, very carefully, I line up a row of ketchup bottles with salt and pepper shakers. "You were all *for* the topic in class last week."

"We were, until we saw how steamed up everyone's getting. It's obvious there's..."

"...gonna be trouble." Lyn finishes all of Stephanie's sentences.

"Look, nobody says the topic's *right*," I explode. "That's why we're discussing it! Anyway, I'm not working on my speech till I get the responses from the questionnaire, so I'll just be a spokesperson for deaf city points of view. Kind of a mouthpiece for the deaf."

"We already get enough of *that* from hearies! Interpreting us all wrong. Telling us what we think..."

"Those speakers are gonna make mincemeat out of you."

I stare at the dead-looking hamburger on my plate and feign horror. "Aaagggh!"

"Don't joke. Some of the speakers are planning their response to your questionnaire before they've even read it and..."

"...*it's not friendly.*"

A shiver runs through me then, but I won't be beaten. "Bee and I've worked too hard on the questionnaire to give up now."

"If that's the way you feel, Lyn'll get Max to protect you..."

"*No one* messes with him!"

The twins give me a "you're crazy" pat (one on each shoulder), wish me luck in unison and take off.

I watch them bounce out of the dining-hall as one. "Why do they have to be so dramatic?"

"Because they're *worried*, you idiot!"

They're not the only ones.

Fact is, I'm scared. The hard lump of fear neither Bee nor I dare admit to kind of puts us off our dinner, and without even discussing it we leave the rest.

The common room is not as crowded as usual because Friday night is movie night. A few kids are lounging around on the sofas or leaning against the Coke machine, but that's about it. On the notice-board is a flyer announcing the Outsiders' trip to the fair at the end of term. If only I could go on it with Joey...

Bee opens our postboxes and empties them. "Hey, Cat. You've got a letter." She brings over a familiar-looking envelope.

"It's from my mum. All my mail's from *her*." Mum has never been my favourite parent, but now I keep remembering the past, I blame her even more. Anyone who leaves her baby to the mercies of nurses with needles doesn't deserve to be high on any popularity list, in my opinion.

Mum's letter is full of her usual forced cheeriness and sappy "I can't believe my little girl's grown up" kind of stuff that makes me want to barf, but today she adds another teaser:

> *I miss you so much, sweetheart. Dad and I are really looking forward to the end of term when we can have our darling girl back home for Christmas.*

Urgh. See what I mean?

And doesn't Mum realize the idea of home to me is about as welcome as an outbreak of measles? It's so lonely there. Nobody signs except Mum and Dad, and Dad's idea of a hilarious sign language joke is to pull his sleeve over his hand like an elephant's trunk and say, "Give the elephant a bun!" Over and over again!

Kids in our neighbourhood act like deafness is catching, and avoid me like the plague. My nursery school friend, Sally, was the only one who stuck by me when I stopped talking. She was fascinated by the novelty of sign language, so, to my mum's undisguised delight, I taught Sally a few words. We'd play together in the holidays, the way little kids can without speaking, and engineer as many situations as possible in which we could use the signs "good", "hi" and "Barbie's bikini" (which, though limiting, seemed to do for us). Then one holiday I came home from school and found Sally had moved away. She wrote to me, but I never replied. (How could I, a six-year-old struggling to learn to read, explain that squiggly marks on a page are even harder to decipher when you can't sound them out loud?)

Suddenly all the rage and confusion about my childhood spurts up inside me into angry bile and I start to compose an imaginary letter to my mum:

> *Dear Mum,*
>
> *Why are you so stupid? Stupid, stupid, STUPID! What makes you think that your everlasting cheerfulness and sugary affection could ever, ever make me forget that you left me? Left me in the hospital. Alone in the silence...*

Caught up in these bitter accusations, I don't immediately notice the common room door open. But when a cool breeze wafts across my legs, I look up and ... to my utter amazement and overwhelming joy...

Heading my way is Joey! All my feelings of rage fly out of the window.

There he is, my fantasy, one hundred per cent real, his tanned skin gorgeous against the white of his T-shirt and the dimpled smile that melts your heart.

I clutch the arm of the sofa, while my stomach competes in the flip-flop Olympics.

"Hi." Joey is using total communication, thank goodness, so at least I'm able to read his signs, if not his lips. "Remember me?" he's saying. "I'm Joey Estrada."

Remember him! The common room recedes into a fuzz of colours and shapes as, hot-faced and trembling, I nod. Strangely enough, even though my conversation is not exactly scintillating, Joey seems to want to stay. "I've not been at deaf city long," he says, leaning his gorgeous body against the wall, "so I don't know anyone outside my classes here... Except *you*."

"Oh."

I can't take my gaze off Joey's eyes crinkling into that leg-melting smile of his. He's talking away, telling me about moving from his last school to deaf city, and I can feel a huge, simple grin split my face in two. I will be the first girl in history ever to die from smiling!

Trouble is, as Joey warms to his subject, he uses less sign and more voice. I try to keep up but I'm unable to understand a word. More than anything I want to respond to Joey, to tell him he's wonderful, gorgeous and desirable, and I'm thrilled to bits he's remembered me, but all I can do is stare at him like an idiot. For the first time in my life, someone I fancy like mad is actually talking to me, and I can't understand what on earth he's saying!

Worse yet, the boy of my dreams has totally forgotten I'm a signer.

Chapter Seven

Finally Joey, realizing something's up, claps his hand to his forehead. "I forgot! You're a *signer*! I'm sorry. When I get excited I sometimes forget to sign."

Excited? Does this boy know the meaning of the word? Excited is when you're watching the boy of your dreams smile at you. Excited is when someone you're attracted to is actually paying attention to you.

"It ... it's OK," I sign shyly.

"It's not OK. I keep forgetting not everyone speech-reads around here. At my last school total communication was law."

"It's supposed to be here too, really. But most of us ignore it." My face feels hot as a chilli pepper as

I try to act normal. "Um. My name is Debbie Katz. My sign name is Cat."

"Cat! Great sign name!" Joey says and he makes the cat gesture like a silent movie villain stroking his moustache.

At this, Bee looks up from the letter she's reading and flashes Joey one of her flirty smiles.

Please, Joey, I know Bee's toffee-coloured hair is lovely and her tawny eyes are to die for, but please like me best, please, *please*.

"Er ... this is my best friend, Bee James. Bee, this is Joey Estrada."

"Hi, Bee James."

"Hi."

Fortunately this is the moment the monster of the silver screen is vanquished in a sea of burning oil and the auditorium spills out a crowd of students discussing the pea-brained creature's downfall.

Jack's crew cut emerges from the crowd and he comes over. "That movie was bad."

"I know," Bee agrees. "We've seen it."

"Who'd be scared by a monster wearing a beret and riding a bicycle?" As Joey makes his signs, he pretends to lose his balance on an imaginary bike.

"Riding a bike?" I smile at Joey. "*That* was the hero."

"They didn't synchronize the subtitles when I saw it at my old school. The hero roared and the monster kept saying 'I love you!'" Joey's expression of mock despair is hilarious.

Jack throws his head back and mimics the monster, pretending Bee's the blonde heroine of the movie. "I love you! I love you!" he tells her and she blushes as we all crack up laughing.

But would Jack be laughing if he knew Joey was a speaker?

Whatever he'd do, Bee's sure to be on his side. She acts like Jack can't put a foot wrong these days. Well, if he can't, neither can Joey.

My heart is starting to jump about again, just as someone waves from the crowd at Joey.

It's Laurie Dean.

Laurie Dean is the most beautiful girl in the school. I watch as she shakes her white-blonde hair and swings her hips as she walks over to Joey. Laurie Dean also happens to be a speaker. "Hi, Joey..." she simpers. "I *mumble mumble*..."

Miserably I watch on the sidelines as Laurie and Joey communicate in voice and sign.

Total communication.

Right now I call it total misery.

And Jack makes it even worse. "Hey," he says, pointing at Joey. "He's a *speaker*!"

"So?"

"So," Jack sneers, "are you using him as research for the debate?"

"Which debate is that?" I snap back, stung by the suggestion. "The one I'm going to win against you or the one you're going to lose against me?"

"Stop it, you two," begs Bee, who wants her boyfriend to get on with her best friend. "Look, Cat, there's Apeman. You said you needed to see him." And she drags me off before I have a chance to retaliate any more.

Apeman, who acts completely differently with speakers, is surrounded by a talking, laughing crowd. He's scratching his chest and bellowing at them like the monster from the movie. We deafies love daft action stuff we can relate to.

"Excuse me, Mr Davis. Excuse me..." Finally I catch his eye. "The Outsiders. Did you talk to Miss Alexander about me becoming a member? I'm participating in the debate so it's important that I join..."

Apeman frowns, and his playful messing about is dropped in an instant. "I heard about the debate, Cat. Unfortunately I've also seen your oral grades."

"I can improve!"

"Well, until I can see something other than Fs in those classes I'm afraid I can't consider you."

"But..."

"Come and see me when you've worked on your grades, Cat."

Fortunately Aggy, entering the common room, saves me from making a rude sign. "What's going on?" she asks.

"Aggy, can we talk privately?"

Aggy nods and motions for me to follow, and as I do, Bee sees something's wrong and leaps up to join us. Thank goodness I can at least rely on my friend.

Inside her office, Aggy switches on the light to reveal a mess of books, papers and cardboard boxes overflowing with Christmas decorations. "Find a space, if you can. The end-of-term committee is trying to work out how to decorate the hall for the Christmas ball."

The ball! The dreaded ball! Bee and I sit amidst chaos, which somehow reflects exactly how I feel.

"Cat. You seem really upset..."

Catching my breath, I burst out, "Mr Davis won't let me into the Outsiders because of my speech-reading grades!"

Aggy's dark brows slant. "Is the Outsiders the reason why you want to change your classes? Mr Kaplan tells me you've asked to get back into the speech-reading programme."

I nod and Bee, sitting beside me, stiffens. This is not the way I planned to break this news to her!

"Is getting back into speech-reading classes part of your research for the debate?"

"We-ell..." Suddenly all the sadness, frustration and crushing disappointment rush into my throat in a choking knot of rage. "Aggy ... I want to be a part of things..."

"Part of what?"

"Everything. The outside world."

"And?"

"And I ... I think ... I want to learn to speak again..."

Bee digs her sharp nails into my arm.

Aggy, unaware of Bee's reaction, asks, "When did this begin, Cat?"

"I don't know really. It kind of started at the

football match. I've been worrying about leaving school at the end of the year and when the fight happened I realized how important it'll be to get on with speakers. Then the Outsiders opened up and..."

"And the debate clinched it?"

"How did you know?"

"I've seen this coming for a long time with you, Cat."

Aggy knew.

She knew, and that's why she made me speak for the motion in the debate.

"At first I thought the only reason I wanted to take speech-reading was for research," I go on, "but now I realize I want to learn to use my voice again no matter what. I want to be able to speak when I leave school and go into the outside world... I ... I can't fool myself any longer..." My hands are trembling.

"Cat, *don't do it*! Don't be a traitor!" cries Bee.

"I won't be."

"You'll be in different classes. We'll hardly see each other. You'll have different friends!"

"It won't make any difference to our friend-ship."

"If you think that, you're blind as well as deaf!"
That hurts.

"Bee, it's just that outside—"

"Outside. Outside. All the time *outside*. You'd think it was heaven the way you talk about it. But it's *hell* out there, and you know it!" Bee's eyes spark with angry tears.

"Come on, Bee," Aggy consoles. "Cat won't be changing all her classes. She'll only have one period of speech-reading a day."

Bee stares out of the window.

"In fact, the information's here somewhere." Aggy riffles through a mess of papers on her desk. "Here it is. Your speech-reading class, Cat, is second period with Mr Davis."

"Mr Davis? But he teaches the year sevens."

"If you want to be in oral classes, you have to catch up."

Catch up with the year seven kids! Disappointed and anxious, I fling a beseeching look at Bee. But she just turns her back on me.

My best friend has turned her back on me!

Is learning to speak really worth this price?

Chapter Eight

That was Friday night, and it doesn't get any better all weekend.

It's a mystery to me why adults go on about the joys of teenage years! What is it for me but a pile of misery? The only boy I've ever liked is probably going out with the most popular girl in the school, I failed to get into the Outsiders and then I got put into a class with a bunch of kids. Now, to top it all, my best friend is acting like I'm a traitor.

By Sunday night I reach fever pitch so I try to calm myself down by sorting out my clothes for school (mind you, with Bee giving me the cold shoulder, it's not easy). Scattered over my bed are the creased-up contents of my drawers – T-shirts, jumpers, jeans and underwear, and I've not even started on my wardrobe. I thought I'd found the answer with my favourite purple top until I spread it out and discovered the memory of a former meal splodged down the front.

Trying to get Bee out of her sulk, I joke, "The only hope for me is to become a nudist!"

Normally Bee would laugh and come up with some clever retort but tonight she just shrugs. She stays huddled in the corner of her bed, as if my side of the room's polluted.

Pretending not to notice, I begin to wheedle. "Bee, can I wear your green top tomorrow? I want to look nice for—"

Bee scowls. "Wear whatever you want. I'm going to sleep. Enjoy your stupid class." She pulls her duvet over her head, leaving her hand sticking out to fingerspell...

"Traitor."

Traitor. As I slump down on my bed, it feels like I've been left to shrivel up and die in some dark lonely place – the same feeling I had when I was a little girl left behind at deaf city.

The next morning, in my first speech-reading class for over a year, the lost lonely feeling is there again, as surrounded by a bunch of year sevens

I watch Apeman take the register.

"Evans, Francis..." Apeman is using total communication. "Oh, and we have a new girl this morning – Debbie Katz."

No one's called me Debbie for years.

The year seven kids, looking like Martians in their oversized headsets, mouth hello to me. Oh my God! If it wasn't for Apeman I'd run, but he's already starting the lesson.

"OK, everyone. This morning we're going to review the *b* and *p* sounds."

At least Apeman is using sign as he speaks. And the *b* sound is one of the easiest to lip-read.

Apeman points to a list of words. "Watch my lips as I read these words: *barber*, *bubble*, *baby*, *Bobby*..."

Swallowing, I concentrate on Apeman's mouth, noting the way the lips meet and push out to make *b*. I'm going to have to watch that mouth for the rest of the year. Big thrill!

"The problem with *b*," Apeman goes on, "is that it is often confused with *p*. Consider the words *bad* and *pad*. With the *p* sound there is a rush of air, but it's impossible to feel it. Unless you're within kissing range." He puckers up and the class giggles.

I immediately think of Joey but I try not to let that distract me.

Apeman is holding up a piece of paper. "When I put this paper in front of my mouth, watch how it moves from the air in the *p* sound. There is no voice with this sound, only air. Now you do it."

I take up my piece of paper and give myself a talking-to which goes something like this: Forget Joey, Debbie Katz. He's a speaker and he's probably speaking right this minute with his beautiful girlfriend. You don't stand a chance with him. And unless you concentrate in this class, you'll never be a speaker either.

Apeman strides from desk to desk making each student say the words. "OK, Cat. *Bad, pad. Big, pig.* Say it."

"*B-b-baa.*" How embarrassing.

"Hit the back of the teeth with your tongue for the *d* ending."

"*D, de, de.*"

"Good, good. Now put the whole thing together. *Bad, bad.*"

"*Baa-de.*" What a slave-driver!

How on earth will I be able to have a normal conversation when I have to concentrate so hard?

"OK, everyone. Practise the *b* sound."

My mouth moves but I'm unable to tell if I'm doing it right. No one will ever be able to read *my* lips!

But Apeman encourages us. "Yes, yes. You're getting it."

Again. Again and again, harder.

"*Barber, bubble, baby, Bobby.*" One whole hour of bubble, bauble, babble.

By the end of the lesson I'm convinced I'll never be able to speak again when just a few silly words exhaust me. But as the others leave, Apeman motions me to his desk. "I'm glad to see you back in a speech-reading class, Cat. As soon as you've improved those grades, we'll see about you joining the Outsiders. But you'll need to practise extra hard to catch up."

"I know."

"Study the vocabulary in this book." Apeman hands me a kid's Early Reader book. "Practise in front of the mirror. Don't worry about getting the sounds right at this point, just your lips."

"Thank you, Mr Davis."

Just then the dividing door between classrooms opens and Aggy bustles in. She looks pretty and flustered in a cardigan and floaty skirt. "Gerry, do you have that clipping about Gallaudet?" Gallaudet is a university for the deaf in America whose students demonstrated because they wanted a deaf president.

"I think I've got it here." Apeman searches through the junk in his desk drawer and finds a newspaper clipping. "Our dear old Alma Mater."

Aggy gives Apeman a soft smile, their eyes meet, then Aggy pulls herself together enough to say to me, "So how was your first class, Cat?"

"OK."

"Cat has worked hard on a questionnaire for the debate," Aggy confides in Apeman as she perches herself on his desk cosily. "Can we see it, Cat?"

"Um, I need to keep the original to make photocopies."

"OK. But let me check it before you hand it out," says Aggy and she turns to Apeman. "Now, Gerry, I wanted to talk to you..."

I leave the two of them to their cosy little chat. Aggy and Apeman? Talk about Beauty and the Beast!

At lunchtime it feels good to get out into the fresh air. The hills look unreal, misty and far away, and the autumn sun is welcoming. Better yet, Bee's waiting for me over by the arts building.

"Bee! I knew you'd come!"

"Do you still want me to go with you to the copy shop?" Despite her sunny yellow shirt, Bee's face is bleak.

"Yeah."

"Did you get permission to go outside?" Bee wants to know.

"Aggy won't mind. Let's just go!"

"Why you can't get copies made at school beats me," moans Bee.

"I want to use their fluorescent paper so it gets noticed."

"It'll get noticed all right," retorts Bee darkly. Then she sighs as if she's made up her mind to sacrifice herself with me. "You'd better help with my lines later on, that's all I can say."

"Anything! Anything!" I hug her and we're friends again.

"I notice," remarks Bee as we make our way over to the bike sheds, "*my* green top looks good with your jeans."

"Thanks! I felt like the Jolly Green Giant in that baby class."

"Yeah. Big, green and stupid."

"Oi!" I pretend to swat Bee, glad to be exchanging insults and messing about again.

But as we reach our bikes I can feel Bee's nerves about going outside, even though it's only to the shops we go to all the time.

"Now for entry into the great unknown," she signs to me, mounting her bike.

"Just call us Armstrong and Shepard. One small step for woman." I swing my leg over my saddle. "One giant step for womankind!" Mounting my bike, I take off alongside her and we shoot down the gravel slope to the main gates, a soft breeze behind us. The avenue ahead looks so pretty, lined with autumn trees and surrounded by the green dented hollows of the hills, that I can't help sighing with pleasure.

Life is not so bad.

But at the copy shop everything changes.

"The place is crowded with hearies," signs Bee, terrified.

"Ignore them." I want to get out too, but I'm determined to do what we came here for. Avoiding any oral communication with the owner of the shop, I simply write down the number of copies and hand it to him with the original. Luckily he's a long-haired back-to-nature type, and he seems to understand. Without any talk he just nods and starts the job. Phew! But when he hands me the thick neat pile of copies, I begin to panic. Our questions seem much more important when they're duplicated four hundred and fifty times.

Worse still, Mr Back to Nature himself is starting to speak. I shake my head to show I don't understand. He pushes back his long hair and repeats himself more slowly this time – as if that does any good.

I wave my hands to show I can't lip-read. I've only just got back into classes!

The owner repeats himself again. He must be shouting now because other people in the shop are staring at us. Embarrassed, Bee grabs a piece of paper. She hands it to the guy and points to a pen.

"Me put on school account?" he writes in pidgin English.

We nod, desperate to get it over with. Why does he have to write in pidgin English? We may be deaf, but we're not stupid. Grabbing the box of questionnaires I make the thank you sign and hurriedly back out of the shop.

"We didn't get permission to charge it to the school," I remind Bee as we mount our bikes.

"The questionnaire's school business, isn't it?"

But as we cycle back to school, I cannot forget how Aggy said that I was opening Pandora's box. Is the box of questionnaires in my basket really that dangerous?

Back at school, the lobby, empty and sunny, is redolent of lunchtime smells and my stomach rumbles with hunger. "Go and grab us some food, Bee. I'll wait here for Aggy."

"OK."

It's a relief to be back here surrounded by familiar sights and smells. Bee's right. The outside is terrifying. Leaning against the big oak table, I finger the top of the pile and begin to reread the questions.

Would you go out with a hearie? Would you marry a hearie?

Suddenly I turn round and there, standing in front of me in the sunlight, is Joey! Joey wearing a shirt so bright it's like he's lit up from inside, and he's smiling right at me.

He's so close I could reach out and touch him. But then I see Laurie Dean sidling up to him. Glamour Puss and Mr Gorgeous. They look so good together. Did I honestly think I stood a chance against someone like that? Someone beautiful, sexy and *oral*?

But I won't give up without a fight. Gently I touch Joey's arm, and he turns to face me.

"Hi, Joey."

"Hi."

"Hi," I repeat stupidly.

"So... What happened to you on Friday night?" Joey asks. "I looked everywhere for you."

Looked for me? As in *wanted to find me*? Feeling my cheeks burn, I sign to him. "The debate. I mean, the questionnaire." I grab a fluorescent sheet. "This. This questionnaire. I mean, I had to talk to Mr Davis."

Joey looks at it, then grins. "Well, I'm glad it wasn't my boring personality!" His eyes twinkle, then they lock into mine. It's like an invisible force field holding us together.

But watching force fields is not Laurie Dean's idea of fun. She demands to see the questionnaire, and before I have a chance to protest she snatches it from my hand.

"Hey! Give that back."

She waves the paper at a group of speakers passing by and shouts something triumphantly. The speakers immediately rush over and suddenly we're overwhelmed by a yelling mob. Pushing and shoving, the speakers try to get hold of copies of the questionnaire.

"Wait a second!" I push the arm of someone who's snatched one from the top of the pile. "Stop, stop!" Another hand grabs a copy, then another. "You're not supposed to see these yet!" But it's hopeless. While I'm using my arms to sign, I can't hold back theirs.

My heart hits my ribcage in painful blows. How will I explain this to Aggy? This wasn't the way she wanted it. And it certainly wasn't what *I* wanted.

But Laurie Dean has got *exactly* what she wanted.

Deaf city's first ever human sacrifice.

Questionnaire

(1) Do you believe total communication is the only way forward?

(2) Do you see sign language as the only true language for the deaf?

(3) Should deafies be integrated into hearing schools?

(4) Should deafies be taught with other handi-capped kids?

(5) How do you feel about hearies governing your country?

(6) How do you feel about hearies leading the world?

(7) Should more deafies become lawyers, doctors, politicians?

(8) Are you tired of telling people to:

   (a) speak one at a time?

   (b) face you?

   (c) repeat their words?

(9) Should everybody, including hearies, be taught sign language?

(10) Would you:

   (a) go out with a hearie?

   (b) have sex with a hearie?

   (c) marry a hearie?

(11) Do you wear your hearing aid big and proud?

(12) Are you glad deafness is the invisible handicap?

(13) Does being deaf sap your confidence?

(14) If you had the chance to become hearing, would you?

(15) Are you ashamed of being deaf?

Chapter Nine

The crowd closes in on me, shoving, grabbing and, worst of all, reading the questionnaire. Now I know how a prisoner feels when his confession's read. *Doomed.*

But one thing's clear. Even if this questionnaire causes a volcanic eruption, it won't bomb. One look at this swarm tells me that.

By now others have joined the crowd, including some signers. Sherry, Myra's hanger-on, with Jude two creeping steps behind, lumbers over and grabs a crumpled copy from the floor.

"What's this rubbish?" Sherry's finger jabs the paper. "Would you have sex with a hearie? Marry a hearie? Who d'you think you are? Hitler?"

Jack, joining in to add his bit, signs, "You've

really let those demons out! Watch me beat you in the debate!"

"I'm going somewhere peaceful to study this," Joey signs to me over everybody's heads.

"Oh. OK." I stare after him as he disappears round the corner with his beautiful speaker. As soon as he reads those questions, he's sure to despise me. Joey, Joey ... I was forced to write those questions. Please don't blame me. I am innocent.

Doomed but innocent...

Gradually the crowd thins out. Even Jude and Sherry have crept away.

Once I saw a documentary about locusts attacking a crop of corn. They came suddenly, a huge black moving cloud, and disappeared moments later. But in that short time they'd stripped every ear of corn to the shafts. That's how I feel. Stripped. Devoured. By a rapacious swarm of students.

Why d'you have to be such a big shot, Cat? How come you didn't ask stupid questions like "Who's your favourite deaf hero?" Cursing my own recklessness, I stash the rest of the questionnaires in my locker and make my way slowly to fifth period – cross-country.

My coach, Miss Zee, is waiting at the track with

her stopwatch round her neck. "Let's improve those times, Cat," she signs enthusiastically during my warm-up. "The regional cross-country finals are only a few weeks away. Myra, watch Cat's start. Yours needs work."

Myra scowls. As if she doesn't detest me enough.

I get into position and when Miss Zee presses her stopwatch, I take off. I'm pushing through the crisp air, running and running, and it feels good.

With each step I leave behind more of the bad feelings, freeing myself from their constraint. I can run. I am powerful. Finally I near the finish where Miss Zee is waiting and nodding encouragement.

Only Myra is displeased with my performance.

Flopping to the ground, chest hammering, I drop my head onto my knees and Miss Zee thumps me on my sweat-prickled back. "Well done, Cat! You beat your own record."

I'm about to give Miss Zee the triumphant smile she expects, when Myra's skinny body blocks out the sunlight behind her. *"Speaker, speaker!"* Myra repeats over and over again with her hands.

That insect!

But she won't beat me down. The power and freedom I felt on the track are still flowing through me. I'm sure now of what I'm doing. If I want to be a speaker no one, least of all Myra, will stop me.

Sixth period is social studies and Apeman's at the classroom door making a big show of checking his watch. Apeman twice a day – what a thrill.

"Turn to page forty-two in your books," he commands the second the light flashes, "and read chapter three."

As I sink into my seat, Bee slips me a pack of cheese crackers.

"Lunch was finished when I got there," she tells me under cover of her desk. "These are all I could get."

"Thanks. I'm starved."

Apeman turns to the board, and hurriedly I unwrap the crackers. Apeman starts to fiddle with his hearing aid. It's just my luck that his aid will amplify the little crackles of the wrapper!

Shoving the cracker and a fair helping of wrapper into my mouth, I open my book to chapter three: "Wars That Changed History". I wonder if the deaf city war will ever make it into the history books...

I'm almost at the end of the chapter when a year seven comes in with a note. It's Jenny, who sat next to me in speech-reading class this morning, and she waves at me like we're best friends.

How embarrassing.

Apeman reads the note and frowns. "You know I disapprove of interruptions, Cat." As if it's my fault!

"Yes, sir."

"Mr Kaplan wishes to see you in his office right away."

Chapter Ten

Usually I like Kaplan's office with its friendly trophies and photographs of deaf city teams (especially the one of me winning the cross-country!).

Usually. Something tells me Kaplan won't be handing out any trophies today.

"You've caused quite a stir with this, young lady." Kaplan points to the piece of paper in front of him.

My questionnaire.

"Who gave you permission to hand these out?"

"I didn't exactly hand them out, sir. Uh, I'm doing a survey for the debate."

"And did Miss Alexander authorize this questionnaire?"

"Um..."

"Did she or did she not authorize this question-naire?" When Kaplan raises his eyebrows like that, it's better to answer.

"I suppose... Yes. No."

"So you handed it out without any author-ization?"

"I couldn't help it. People grabbed them from me. It happened so fast." I lower my head and with one finger trace the stitching on my jeans, over and over again. I don't know where to look.

Kaplan leans over and pulls my head up to face him. "Young lady, it's not that I think you've done anything wrong asking these questions. They're points that you need to bring out in the debate and for the *most* part they are reasonable issues for young hearing-impaired people..."

If he mentions the sex question I'll die of embar-rassment.

"But the whole thing is like pouring fuel on a fire."

And guess who's going to burn.

"To bring these things out needs sensitivity, concern..."

And a flameproof suit.

"They should be talked about in a civilized manner. By a teacher."

"So why hasn't a teacher done it?" I can't help blurting it out.

Kaplan fixes me with one of his looks. "You know our aim here is to use total communication."

Same old speech.

"We believe using manual and oral communication combined is the best way for the hearing impaired to assimilate in the hearing world."

"I know, sir. But not everybody here wants total communication, so I asked those questions..."

"Of course, we don't wish to force anyone. But we've seen the results with other schools. We know what's best for our pupils." Kaplan gets up and goes to the window to stare out. Against the brilliant light his hair sticks out, making him look like some kind of mad scientist.

Suddenly he spins round. "The debate will be conducted with the usual procedures?"

"Yes."

"I will speak with Miss Alexander. In the meantime ... *don't* hand out any more questionnaires, Cat."

"No, sir."

Bee is waiting for me in the corridor, a pent-up figure of tension. "I knew it was bad news opening up this stuff," she cries. "I never wanted to do it in the *first* place!"

"Too late now. Will you come with me to get the rest of the questionnaires from my locker? Kaplan says not to pass out any more."

"Cat, please pull out of the debate before it's too late."

"I can't."

There's a bewildered line to Bee's mouth. "I don't understand you any more, Cat. You're like a different person."

"Nothing has changed between *us,* Bee."

"Dream on." Bee shakes her head and we make our way over to the lockers without another word. More and more lately there's this uncomfortable sense of distance between us. A tiny crack, splitting, widening like a chasm.

At the lockers I fiddle with my combination lock, but there's something wrong with it today. With an effort I force the lock to click to the right and suddenly it snaps apart and the door swings open. Inside is a messy pile of papers, shoved in haphazardly, but then my hand, scrabbling in the dark

90

recesses of the locker, touches something soft and squidgy.

Something furry...

And it *moves.*

"Aaagh!" I wrench my hand away and the force knocks me to the floor in a shower of papers. *"Aaagh! Aaagh!"* I shriek as I see, dangling from my locker, the hairy-legged body of an enormous tarantula!

"It's OK, Cat. It's only a fake!"

"But ... but it *moved.*"

Bee takes the attached string between her thumb and finger and traces it to the door. "No wonder! *Now* will you give up?"

But before I've time to reply, Jack bursts into the lobby, red-faced and panting. "Someone get Kaplan! There's a *fight*!"

Bee's eyes meet mine. We both hate fights, but at deaf city you can't ignore them.

Outside, kids are running towards the arts building from all directions, and as we race round the corner we see a crowd gathering on a grassy mound. In the middle of an angry challenging mob, two bodies are rolling in the dirt. It's Max and Sammy Jackson, a weasel-like speaker who's always causing trouble.

"They're fighting over your questionnaire," Myra Ryder informs me with grim satisfaction.

"What?!"

"Sammy said your questionnaire was garbage, and Max told him to keep his stupid speaker mouth shut, so Sammy said Max was a retard signer who needed a brain transplant. Max said, 'Wanna donate your weasel brain, speaker?' so Sammy said, 'Yeah' and they started to fight."

"Oh no..."

Suddenly Kaplan arrives on the scene and barrels his way through the crowd, closely followed by Apeman. They grab the boys by their collars and with brute strength pull them to their feet. Kaplan almost has to stand on tiptoe to do it.

Panting, Max reins in an almighty punch, his massive power held in check by sheer force. Sammy pushes his shaggy hair out of his face and wipes a bloody nose with the back of his hand, his eyes flashing sour hatred.

"It's my fault," I cry. "I've got to tell Kaplan. It's all my fault."

"Don't flatter yourself," Jack says. "This is an old fight."

"And you could get suspended," Bee points out to me.

Bee's right. For a second I think of what suspension would mean. Being banned from sport, maybe even the debate. Losing Joey for good (with me off the scene Laurie Dean could really make a move on him) and being a complete and utter failure in everything that matters to me.

What a mess.

Sighing, I make a colossal effort to push these horrors aside and work on gathering my courage. "I *have* to explain ... I just have to..." I repeat over and over as I watch Kaplan's stocky figure march the fighters in.

"Max wouldn't thank you if you interfered," Bee warns me.

Since Lyn's plea for my protection, Max has been my unofficial minder, and as my minder losing face would be worse than anything, Bee insists. In fact, Bee insists and argues so much that when I heroically persist with my need to explain to Kaplan, she grabs my shoulders hard enough for her nails to dig into my flesh. "I'm sick of you playing the hero, Cat! Can't you see it's breaking us up? You and me. Us ... deaf city. Breaking *everything* up!

Quit the debate right now!"

"I can't."

"You'll be sorry if you don't."

Chapter Eleven

But I can't quit.

When questionnaires scrawled with obscene comments are scattered across the school like stray fire bombs, I can't quit. When everyone, including Joey – *especially Joey!* – avoids me as if I'm contaminated, I still can't quit. Even when my best friend acts like I've betrayed her, something won't let me give up.

Ironically the issue at the root of all the problems – the questionnaire – is the very thing which drives me on. There's a force stronger than me at work here. A power building in the completed questionnaires, fuelled by the secret hopes and feelings of so many deaf kids. It's a power too great to ignore. It shows in their answers and in the many personal messages to me. Messages like: *Wish I had your guts* or:

> I'm desperate to become a signer because since I lost the last of my hearing, it's so much easier to sign. Sign language is the most beautiful, expressive language and it's ours. Trouble is, I'm scared to lose my speaker friends.

Another one says: *Don't agree with your stand, but glad this stuff is coming out.*

Out there are kids who want this debate.

They may not be trailing after me with banners and cheers, but they support me and, secretly, some are even hoping I'll win. One little girl sent me a whole letter:

> Dear Debbie Katz,
>
> I think God should make everyone deaf so they'd know what it feels like. Not for ever, because people would get knocked down by cars and stuff, but just for a little while. When they woke up hearing they would say, "Wow, this is nice." But they

96

would remember how it felt to be deaf.
When I grow up, I'm going to be a scientist
so I can work on a drug to make hearing
kids deaf and another one to make deaf
kids hear. Then kids can choose what they
want.

Love Sandy
PS: I know Aggy told us not to sign our
questionnaires, but I'm not ashamed to let
people know how I feel.

There's something about Sandy's courage and faith in me that gives me heart.

Choosing is what it's all about. Choosing how to communicate.

If only my best friend could see this!

It's hard to do the usual everyday things without Bee. She tells me it's because she's involved with rehearsals, but the truth is she can't forgive me for refusing to quit. These days I even go to the dining-hall early because the pain of eating alone is so much easier to bear when the place is empty.

But tonight, as I reach the swing doors, I see the dining-hall is not empty.

Joey is in there. And he's alone.

Do I dare approach him? Do I dare risk rejection? I turn away. But when will I get another chance like this? Laurie Dean is stuck to him like glue these days, so it may be my only opportunity to see him alone.

Taking a very deep breath, moistening my lips and fluffing out my hair, I turn round, push open the swing doors and slowly, slowly walk across the long, long hall right up to him.

"Hello, Joey," I sign falteringly.

"Cat!" he signs as if the major war in deaf city history is not happening. "Looks like we can be the first to guess tonight's mystery meat."

"What a treat." I line up with Joey and with trembling hands load a tray, hardly noticing what I'm putting on it. Chicken, carrots, salad and green jelly, green jelly. Whoops, put some back! Is this really happening? Is this me? As I lead the way over to a corner table, my heart is thumping away like a mad thing, and when Joey sits down opposite me, I think it'll burst.

Does this mean things are OK with us? That he hasn't been avoiding me?

It must do. It must because when he sits down

98

to eat, Joey is as natural as anything, even – dare I say it – *cheerful.*

"I'm pleased to announce tonight's mystery meat is not dried cat food, but real non-CJD beef!" he announces after his first mouthful. "At my last school we had to sue the cook under the Food Descriptions Act."

I laugh in a great gush (the release is so great) and the spring inside me uncurls a tiny notch. "You should've been here before the food riots," I counter, picking up on Joey's spirited conversation. "Things came to a head when Kaplan got caught in the middle of one of the riots. He objected to wearing leftovers. Something to do with the colour combo of peas and beans not being to his *taste.*"

"Taste!" Joey grins at my pun, then makes one of his own. "What a *riot*!"

We laugh together for a moment or two, then out of the blue Joey gets surprisingly serious. "Riots are OK, Cat, but I reckon your way of settling disputes is better."

"It is?"

"Definitely. You hit home on all the issues. I've been working on an essay about deaf rights, but

I just couldn't get my ideas organized until I read your questionnaire. Then suddenly it all fitted into place."

Does this guy take lessons in gorgeousness?

The nerves fall away from me completely then and it's just Joey and me, talking, signing, laughing and sharing ideas. Joey tells me all about how he wants to become deaf city's first ever professor of languages. He says he's doing a study of sign in different languages and it's fascinating how different and yet similar sign is in various languages. Joey's enthusiasm is catching, and I tell him how I plan to be deaf city's first ever lawyer, which seems to impress him no end.

It's the best meal I've ever allowed to go cold.

Unfortunately it doesn't last. Just as Joey's about to share some of his rapidly melting ice cream with me, I see Laurie Dean heading our way. Glamour Puss is surrounded by an adoring crowd of speakers, and they're all talking like mad.

Great.

"Hi, Joey. Mind if we sit here?" she simpers, twitching her cute little bottom as she sits down beside him – and it doesn't take a degree in speech-reading to understand *that* message!

Joey smiles at her. Of course he smiles at her! She's the most beautiful girl in the school, isn't she? I'm just the lanky signer he jokes with while he's waiting for her. He says something to her and she giggles flirtatiously, her pink glossy mouth answering back. Laurie makes a perfect dessert in her ice-cream-coloured top and tight pink jeans. Trouble is, she doesn't melt away.

Chapter Twelve

Joey fingerspells Laurie's name as she unloads her tray and Laurie moves her glossy lips in reply. Not for this deafie the clumsiness of signing!

The other speakers sit down now, amidst general chatting and laughter (which, of course, is gibberish to me). The dining-hall has shrunk to a bunch of speaker faces mouthing silent words.

What are they saying?

Why don't they try to include me? Has my skin turned green? Have I sprouted horns? Selfish speakers! How could I have forgotten that Joey is one of them?

But Joey does something so incredible right then, he proves he's different. Using speech and sign combined he says, "Can we stick to total communication, guys? Cat here's a signer."

Sammy Jackson, the troublemaker who fought Max, points at me. "You're the signer who did that questionnaire."

"For the debate that will bring deaf city together!" I retort.

"Who wants to be 'together' with a bunch of signers?"

Joey cuts in. "At my school back home we all used total communication."

"This isn't 'back home'!" snorts Sammy.

"That's for sure!"

The air bristles with hostility. Finally Laurie signs to me, patronizingly slowly, "So, don't *you* agree that signers and speakers should go to separate schools?"

"I'm working on my answer to that for the debate."

"Debate," sneers a guy in a baseball cap. "More like *war*. Sammy's fight proved it."

Heat floods up my neck, burning my face red. "All the fight proved was that we need to get things into the open..."

Laurie smirks at me and delivers her barb. "Don't *you* speech-read at all?" she enquires, all sweetness and innocence.

"I ... I ... I'm taking classes with Mr Davis."

"Mr *Davis*? But he only teaches year *sevens*."

"I ... I need to catch up."

"Oh. I *see*." From under her curled lashes, Laurie decides I'm no threat to someone like her, and turns back to Joey. Naturally he's all eyes.

How can I compete with looks, bitchiness *and* a mouth that speaks?

"I have to go. I have to go now." I jump up. "I've got training." Tears throbbing behind my eyes, I bolt out of the dining-hall, leaving Joey and the speakers staring open-mouthed after me.

The deserted track stretches out invitingly and, taking off like a bullet, I run and run. On the track I am ME. Not a label – not deaf or hearing, not speaker or signer – just ME. Just me, me, me running ... faster and faster. Held-back tears now sting my cheeks as a terrible thought beats in time with my legs. *Speakers and signers don't mix. Don't mix ... don't mix...* Panting, I round the far corner of the track to see somebody waving to me up ahead.

Squinting against the sun, I make out the tanned arms of Joey signing to me. Even from far away

104

I can see what he's saying. "Hey, Cat! D'you want a speech-reading coach?"

Speech-reading coach?

"My fees are the lowest in town."

Gulping air as I reach him, I slow down and joyfully sign back, "You're hired!"

Nothing can upset me now. Not even Myra, who's stopped her warm-up exercises to stare at us. Joey wants to help me! He wants to help me learn to speak.

Nothing can hurt me now.

Chapter Thirteen

Next night, infused with renewed enthusiasm, I'm making a chart for the questionnaire responses, while Bee lounges on her bed, reading a book. Once my best friend and I did nothing but laugh and mess about, but tonight I'm grateful for the uneasy truce we've struck.

Suddenly our room buzzer flashes – two short bursts. "It's for you," says Bee, nudging me with her toe. Someone wants me on the minicom. Probably my mum.

But what if it's an enemy? A caller on the minicom, the telephone for the deaf, has no voice, no sound, just typed words on a screen. The messenger can remain totally anonymous. Nervously I lift up the receiver and watch the words slowly crawl across the screen. R u THERE. CAT? R u THERE?

WHO IS IT? I type back, full of dread.

C ... O ... crawls across the screen. My heart squeezes as the letters A, C and H quickly follow. Coach who?

EST... Suddenly everything is wonderful because I know what the next letters are: R A D A.

HI. JOEY.

HI. R u READY FOR YOUR FIRST LESSON?

YEAH.

MEET YOU OUTSIDE THE ORAL LABS AT EIGHT.

OK.

Does Joey know the risk we're taking — a signer and a speaker meeting at the oral labs after hours? It's impossible to tell from a minicom message, not being able to see a face or, like a hearing person on the phone, hear expression in a voice.

C u THERE! Joey types and is gone before I can say any more.

"Who was it?" Bee wants to know when I burst back into our room.

"Joey Estrada."

"Joey?"

"Yes. He wants to meet me at the oral labs." I might as well spill *all* the beans. "Don't tell anyone, Bee, but he's going to help me with my speech-reading."

Slowly, very slowly, Bee smooths out the creases on her bedcover. "Doesn't Joey know it's death for a speaker and a signer to meet?" she asks finally.

I shrug.

"Since Max's fight, it's all-out war. You can't go out with him."

"I'm not going out with him. It's just a speech-reading lesson."

Bee looks at me, and her tawny eyes narrow. "Deaf city is full of spies. If signers and speakers are seen *smiling* at each other, word gets around these days. You're asking for trouble, Cat."

"Look, I'm not exactly mad about spiders or spiteful gossip, but I really like Joey, Bee. Can't you understand?"

Bee shrugs and goes back to her book as if she can't be bothered to answer. "It's your funeral," she signs.

That hurts.

Why does my best friend have to act this way? I know she's worried about me, but can't she be on my side like she always used to be? It's making everything so much worse. Well, it's not going to spoil the closest thing to a date this teenager's ever had!

But as I sneak down the back staircase to meet Joey, I can't help feeling very mixed up. Inside I'm hurt yet excited, happy yet scared, and totally at the mercy of others (mostly enemies!). Halfway down the stairs I check my reflection in the window and pull my shirt out of my jeans. Best to keep the size of my breasts (so much smaller than Laurie's) a mystery for as long as possible.

Joey is waiting outside the labs, wearing his heart-stopping smile, but I don't have time to greet him because at that very moment Myra Ryder jogs round the corner. I give Joey a warning look, but luckily Myra ignores us and runs by in her black tracksuit as if we're some lower form of pond life.

"Maybe she didn't see you," I sign hopefully. But spiders have peripheral vision.

"Come on," says Joey firmly. "We've got work to do." As if the lab didn't publicize the fact! On the walls, charts of oversized lips forming sounds remind me of why we're here. If mouths really looked that gross, kissing would die out overnight!

Joey motions me to sit down, all business.

Romance with a speaker.

What a hope.

Chapter Fourteen

The oral labs are sweltering. The evening sun beats mercilessly through the row of closed windows, bouncing off the mirrors and warming the sweating vinyl stools. But it's too risky to open the windows – someone might notice them. In the mirrored cubicle I take the headset Joey offers me, but as I lower it over my head, my hair, like my feelings, is flattened.

Some date.

"Let's start with the *br* sounds." Joey has my copy of *Lip Lessons* open in front of him. "OK, when I make that sound, see how my tongue rests against the back of my teeth?"

I nod, mesmerized by Joey's even white teeth.

"Try it, Cat."

Feeling horribly embarrassed, I purse my lips.

"No, no. Curl in the lips tighter and let the air out in a rush. Look at my lips."

How can I not? Lips like Joey's should be reserved for kissing.

"There's something wrong, Cat. You're not rolling in your bottom lip far enough. Watch mine in the mirror."

I try to copy Joey, but it feels like my lips have been chipped from something rock solid and I can't move them properly. "*Brr ... brrruh, brrrah, brrrr.*"

"Feel the rush of air against your fingers." Joey takes my fingers and places them against his mouth. "See?"

Someone nods. I think it's me.

"Try it again." Joey puts his fingers to my lips to feel if I'm doing it right.

His eyes hold mine as I make the sound.

"OK. You've got it."

I certainly have. We stare at each other. Our images, reflected over and over in the enclosed space, stare back. Somewhere in my chest a heart thuds. Without a sign, Joey takes my hand to his mouth and repeats the sound against it, over and over again. Only his lips move and then, gently, gently, he begins to kiss my fingertips.

My insides tighten at the touch of his soft, gentle lips. The mirrored cubicle has become our own shining world and we're lost in the best speech-reading lesson of my entire life.

Until a dark shadow falls across us.

Myra. Myra Ryder reflected over and over again in the mirrors, blotting out every scrap of light. I don't know how long she's been watching us, but her look of sulky malevolence says she's seen enough. Her bony shoulders give an exaggerated shrug and she turns on her heel and slams out the door. She's got what she wanted.

"We've got to get out of here!" With shaking hands I pull off the headset. "Myra will be gathering a lynch mob right now. Say you were forced to do it, Joey."

"Forced to do what? Kiss your hand?"

"No, no. Forced to teach me." I tug his arm. "Come *on*."

"Why let her scare us?" Joey says, removing his headset too.

"Joey, you don't know Myra. She ... she hates me. She has it in for me because I beat her at cross-country. She'll do anything to get back at me. Let's hurry."

But it's already too late. Marching down the hall is Myra with her willing slaves, Jude and Sherry. Like an advancing pack of marionettes, they sign in unison. "Speaker! Speaker!"

In defiant protection, Joey puts an arm across my shoulders, incensing my attackers even more.

"Speaker! Speaker!" Their signs cut the air. "Speaker! Speaker!" They gesture over and over again.

Then, with sly triumph, Myra holds out her left hand and waggles her right fingers inside it like a wiggling tongue inside a mouth. "Forget your Cat nickname," she sneers. "That's your new sign name."

It's not a name that can be translated into words – just a horrible, horrible sign with the hand in a c shape for my name and the wiggling tongue of a speaker inside it. But its ugly meaning is all too easy to read. Myra's had to live down the sign name Spider and she knows how much it hurts to be given a cruel sign name. She really wants to hurt me.

Seeing the impact this has on me, Joey has a

message of his own. "Cat," he signs in big, defiant gestures. "Cat, will you come with me on the Outsiders' trip?"

My enemies stare, their signs frozen in mid-air.

"Come with me to the fair. If you're in the speech-reading programme you can join the Outsiders."

Oh, Joey, how I'd love to go with you...

Of course, agreeing to go is public death.

But, forming my hand in the sign that is almost fistlike, I jerk it forward over and over.

"Yes! Yes! YES!"

Chapter Fifteen

"You agreed to go with Joey on the Outsiders' trip? With Myra and her gang as witnesses?" Bee, standing in the middle of the dorm kitchen, is astounded by my news. "Cat ... you must be insane."

"I am. Insanely in love..." I can't stop smiling. The last half-hour with Joey has made me so happy. Too happy to let Bee or even the whole of deaf city get me down.

But Bee is determined to do her best. "Even if you're in love with a speaker, do you need to broadcast it over the whole of deaf city?"

Yes, I do, I tell Bee with my face. *The boy of my dreams asked me out. He kissed my hand. He likes me!*

Bee protests, but I grab her hands and drag her

around the kitchen in a whooping dance of joy, banging into cabinets and chairs like a lunatic. Eventually Bee just has to laugh.

"Cat, you're mad..."

Maybe I am mad, but how can I resist Joey? I've never known a boy so funny and yet so thoughtful and serious before. A boy so completely kind and brave and caring. He's just the type of person I've always dreamed about. In bed that night, I fantasize about going out with Joey. I picture him kissing my fingertips, my hands, my arms, my neck ... and then my mouth...

Suddenly the darkened ceiling of our room is illuminated by a hard beam of light snaking its way across in looping letters. A torch is writing a secret message, and there's no doubt it's for me:

W-A-T-C-H O-U-T T-R-A-I-T-O-R

Pulling my duvet over my head, I burrow down into the deep, safe in the darkness of my bed, and huddle up there, alone with the drumming of my heart. I'm scared. Very scared. Who is threatening me and what do they plan to do?

When I eventually drift off into a fitful sleep,

I'm tortured by horrific nightmares. Small and abandoned in a dark forest, I'm chased by a huge predator which creeps after me through the menacing shadows.

"Mummy! Mummy!" I scream but no sound comes out. Frantic with terror I trip, and the predator inches towards me...

I wake up sweating and screaming, with a damp rope of hair stuffed in my mouth. I spit it out and, shaking, stumble over to the sink to splash my face with cold water. A thin yellow light is seeping through the curtains.

No point in trying to get back to sleep now.

The only comfort is that no threat towards me can ever be as bad as my own dreams.

In first period, deaf culture, my brain feels clogged and my eyes sore. But I'm awake enough to notice the new flyer on the wall advertising the debate, and somehow it feels like a death sentence.

"Cat, are you with us?" Aggy's perfume wafts over me as she touches my shoulder. "Bring your chair over to the circle." Just my luck it's circle time, where it's impossible to sneak a catnap. "We're discussing why in the past the deaf have been labelled retarded," signs Aggy, perching on the corner of her desk. "One of the reasons the deaf appear strange is their exaggerated facial expressions." Aggy mimics a grimace, and the class laughs. "But these faces can be embarrassing for hearing people. How does everybody here feel about that?"

For a moment no one answers, then Myra, seated on one side of me, renews her attack with that horrible waggling tongue sign name (under cover of her notebook, of course).

"Did you say something, Myra?" enquires Aggy.

Myra shifts in her seat. "Uh ... I was just saying... Signers who learn to speak are traitors."

"Hearies should learn to sign instead," asserts Megan Gerard.

Jack cuts in, serious for once. "No way. Sign language is *our* language. My parents brought me up to respect sign language. It's not" – Jack looks embarrassed at his own intensity – "some, some *lightweight* thing do-gooder hearies should try to impress people with."

"You have a point, Jack. What do you think, Cat?"

Eleven faces turn to look at me. I glance down

and fiddle with my pencil case, but then, remembering the way Joey put his arm round me when I was surrounded by Myra's gang, I find the guts to say, "I think the more people who learn sign language the better."

Bee gives me a half-smile (I used to get full smiles from my best friend) and others join in with the discussion. Despite their enthusiasm, the lesson drags and it's a relief when the light flashes for second period.

In speech-reading, Apeman notices me drifting and waves his hands in front of my face. "Hey, miss, you're supposed to be catching up, not dreaming!" he says.

No big deal, but for some reason I want to cry. If only I could move on from these baby classes, with the ugly wallcharts and fidgety little kids.

"Jenny!" I sign as my neighbour shakes the desk for the umpteenth time. "You nearly knocked my book off!"

Jenny crosses her knees and gives me a pained expression. "But I need to go to the toilet."

"Apeman will let you go."

Jenny shakes her head. "Signers..."

Eventually the light flashes for breaktime, and

as Apeman signals for us to pack up, I ask, "What about signers?"

"They wait for us when no one else is about," Jenny explains, backing hurriedly out of the door. "They make horrible signs at us – torment us." And with that she hurtles to the toilet.

So the deaf city war has hotted up.

I remember how it felt to be bullied in year seven. (The war between signers and speakers has been going on for ever.) I've always been tall for my age but despite this I still felt afraid of gangs of speakers who loved to torment us. They made us signers feel stupid and were always teasing us when teachers weren't around. Seems that now signers are doing the same.

It's such a horrible morning, it's a relief to get to training. Miss Zee is giving us one of her pep talks. "OK, remember to pace yourselves. Don't use up all your energy in the first ten minutes. You'll need some for that final push."

OK.

"Right, once round the track for a warm-up." Miss Zee blows her whistle and we take off.

One two, one two, breathe in. One two, one two, breathe out. The sluggish heaviness weighing me down is melting away with each breath. One two, one two, breathe in... I picture each footfall as a battle in the deaf city war. If only I could run through the obstacles in my life this easily!

"Good," signs Miss Zee as we finish. She motions to Myra. "Myra, don't overdo it at the start. You need to pace yourself like Cat."

Myra shoots me a look of venom. *Oh, great.*

"OK." Miss Zee checks her stopwatch. "Give me a good half-hour run across the fields and through the woods. Ready, steady, GO!"

One two, one two, breathe in. One two, one two, breathe out. We head out for the woods surrounding the playing fields.

It feels good.

Who cares about Myra? She's pacing herself but still ahead of me, leading the way. OK, Myra Ryder, lead the way, but I'll catch up with you! Just you see. I'm feeling confident and fast.

I'm going well as I enter the woods, when suddenly my shin slams against something sharp and hard with a sickening force. *Thwack!*

"Aaaagh!" I go flying and crash to the ground. And as I lie there, my whole body radiating pain, I can see, glinting menacingly in the sunlight, a long steel bar. It's a high jump bar and it's been carefully concealed with foliage and wedged between two trees. Blood oozes down my throbbing leg and soaks my socks, but all I can think is…

Was it put there for me?

Chapter Sixteen

"Let's see the damage, Cat," demands Miss Zee, running over.

Gingerly I lift up my sticky wet hand to reveal a deep gash slicing right across my shin.

"Ouch!"

"I think you'll need stitches there."

"But the regional finals are coming up soon!"

Miss Zee looks as upset as I feel. "I'm afraid you'll have to let that heal first, Cat. Come on. Let me help you up and get you to the infirmary."

"I won't have to go to hospital, will I?" I sign, sick at the thought.

Miss Zee's surprised to find someone as big as me scared of hospitals. "Cat, don't worry. Stitches are not that bad."

How can I explain that it's not just the stitches? It's the thought of the antiseptic smell ... those white coats ... those cold, efficient hands...

An hour later, in the brilliantly lit hospital waiting-room, the antiseptic smell is suffocating. Clutching the arms of my wheelchair, I feel small and scared and alone.

Without warning, someone in green overalls grabs my wheelchair from behind and whisks me away. Maybe he's explaining to me where we're going, but deaf kids who can't read lips have to rely on gut reaction, and my gut reaction's now shaking my whole body and shooting sparks of terror from me as it sends the world spinning into a fuzz of electric colours. In the examining room a frenzied fear closes in on me, sucking me up in its merciless, terrible wake. I scream and struggle as firm, efficient hands hold me down. Suddenly I'm five years old again and very, very sick...

A white-coated nurse, her head a tiny pink bead, drifts high above me, very far off. She's smaller than a pinprick but her hands are so big they can reach me way, way up here on my floating, faraway bed, and pierce me with their giant needle.

"Mummy! *Mummy!*" I scream and scream, but no sound comes out. There is only silence – silence sifting in great cold flakes into an infinite abyss of more silence.

My mother has left me alone in the silence.

As I wake from a fitful doze, my mum's face swims into focus in front of me. The expression of anxiety, love and concern is exactly as I remember it that other terrible time. And all the frightening and sad feelings come flooding back. "Don't leave me again, Mum. Don't leave..."

"OK, darling."

Hours or minutes later (time, somehow, gets all squashed up and stretched out like a concertina) Mum is still there. Then, rearing up from the confused jumble inside my head, my inhibitions are released, and I ask the question. The big, burning question I've never ever dared ask before. "Mum ... why ... *why did you leave me*?"

"I'm still here, Debbie."

"No, before..."

"I got here as soon as I could."

"No, no. *Before.* When I was little ... in hospital. I called and called but ... you never came..."

Mum doesn't answer right away. Then in halting signs, with the painful memories etched across her face, she tells me. "When your fever got so dangerously high, they made me wait outside your room... I didn't want to, but they made me. I waited outside in that draughty corridor for hours and hours. It was awful, trying to imagine what was going on behind that closed door with my little girl. I was always right there. I would never *ever* leave you."

"So you didn't go?"

"No. I never went."

The soft and complete relief washes over me like a cleansing and refreshing rain. The blessed relief of finally knowing my own mother never abandoned me rocks me gently in and out of sleep.

I squeeze her hand in thanks. "Oh ... good. Good ... good ... goodnight, Mum."

"Goodnight, sweetheart."

Chapter Seventeen

My leg needed six stitches. I don't know how loud my screams were, but word is I left permanent dents on the examining table from the kicking.

How humiliating.

Back at deaf city I'm allowed to miss classes, but after one whole day and a half of being stuck in my room wrestling with my debate speech, I'm going mad. I've been so unnerved by my so-called accident that I can't sort my thoughts out for the speech. So at lunchtime I get up and hobble over to the dining-hall to find Bee.

"I had cabin fever in our room," I tell her as I prop my leg up on a chair.

"Poor Cat," Bee consoles. "Let me get you some lunch."

"Thanks."

Bee is being extra nice to me since my accident. She picks out all my favourite things to eat and brings a loaded tray over to me.

Max and Lyn are hot on her heels.

"Who did it?" Max asks, pointing to my leg.

I shrug.

He ponders this. "Yeah, well... I'll get whoever did it, anyway."

"Look. I appreciate it, Max. But I don't want any more trouble. It was probably an accident."

"Oh, let her take care of herself!" retorts Lyn and she pulls on her boyfriend's arm. "Come on." Together they take off.

And I'd thought Lyn was my friend.

"With friends like that, who needs enemies?" I say, doing my best to make light of Lyn's defection.

But Bee's reply is unexpectedly unsympathetic. "You're lucky to have Max on your side."

"What d'you mean?"

"I didn't want to tell you this, Cat," Bee sighs, "but Jack says some of the boys are pretty steamed up about you going out with a speaker. You know they reckon signer girls belong to them."

"I'm not their property."

"But signers always stick together. Anyway, you never know, maybe Dave Grant's going to ask you out."

"Dave Grant? But he's never even spoken to me!"

"I think he's going to ask you, just the same. A couple of the boys were talking about taking you to the Christmas ball..."

"Why all of a sudden...?" Suddenly an ugly realization dawns on me. "I get it! They want me tied up so I can't go with Joey." And I know I've hit on the truth from Bee's ashamed look.

"It ... it wasn't exactly like that."

"Yeah, right!" Something hot and tight inside me thrusts to get free. "I was Miss Wallflower of deaf city until Joey noticed me! I don't want any favours from signer boys."

"Cat, if you had a signer boyfriend we could double date," Bee urges. "We'd have fun together again. Like before." The allusion that everything has changed between us is not lost on me and that really hurts.

I try to explain. "Bee, I know I'm a signer, but I can go out with a speaker if I want to. And I *do* want to! I want Joey. And he wants me. I'm learning to speak again with him. And ... it's all coming back to me. The way it felt to open my mouth and speak ... the way it felt to... Well, I love it, Bee! I love being with Joey and I love learning to talk."

"I've noticed."

"I'm sorry, Bee. Deaf city code is not the law."

"But it's *our* law, just the same. And going out with the enemy isn't going to help." Bee leans over and squeezes my hand. "I'm sorry too, Cat. But someone had to tell you. I do care about you, you know."

"I know." I try to smile gratefully at Bee but all I can think of is how I'm the booby prize in the date stakes. Am I really that unattractive?

When the light flashes for fifth period, Bee gives me a parting hug and I hobble out of the dining-hall to have another crack at my speech before my speech-reading lesson with Joey. Let Myra win the cross-country. I'm out of the competition now.

As I reach the big walnut tree at the back of the science block where I'm due to meet Joey, I remember how I hated the fact that signer boys could never be more than friends to me.

131

Well, now they're not even that!

Easing myself down carefully, I arrange my stiff leg on the grass, glad to get away from the signer boys' vicious games. The ironic thing is, Joey's supposed to be the enemy, but these days he's the only person I can rely on. I prop myself against the tree trunk and stare up through the branches to the sky. If only my problems could float up through those branches and dissolve in the blueness up there.

Everything's such a mess.

In the distance a group of speakers are cutting across the field to the science block, talking, gesturing. They look friendly and completely at ease. Why should they be my enemies? We're all deaf, aren't we?

Then it hits me.

At deaf city we're always going on about the prejudice of hearies against deafies, but we're just as bad! Isn't it prejudice not to let someone change their mind about how they talk? Prejudice not to let speakers and signers mix?

Suddenly inspired, I grab my notebook and begin to write my speech:

132

Deaf kids everywhere, don't be the victims of prejudice!

And the words spill out from me like an avalanche:

Do you want to live in a deaf ghetto for the rest of your life? A ghetto full of suspicion and hatred? If you do, you must never go on the outside.

Line after line scrawls across the page – everything I want to say:

People can't understand us. Hearing people act as interpreters. Sometimes they don't translate exactly what we want to say and this frustrates us...

I'm concentrating so hard I don't see Joey until he's right in front of me.

"How's the leg?"

"What? Oh…" I smile up at him. "Throbs a bit. The worst part is letting down the team. Still … one more day of missing cross-country and I'll have the whole debate speech finished. I think I'm getting a handle on it at last."

"I'm glad you're going ahead with it." Joey sits down next to me. "Deaf city has a lot to learn about the deaf community."

"But deaf city *is* the deaf community!"

Joey shakes his head. "The deaf community is *all* deaf people, and there are lots of different attitudes to the ones around here."

"Like what?"

"Like 'everyone should be oral because it makes things easier outside'."

"But if you're born deaf, it's not as easy to speak as it is when you're hard of hearing."

"I was born deaf."

"You!" Because Joey's oral, I'd assumed he lost his hearing after he'd learned to speak, like I did. "But, Joey, you talk so well!"

"That's what you think! You can't hear my voice, and according to my little brother I sound like a robot."

I smile. "But robots are the men of the future."

"Thank you." Joey pretends to be a robot and signs with jerky movements, "Rea-dy ... for ... your

... next ... less-on ... my little ... droid?"

I laugh. "Whatever you say, R2-D2."

Joey opens the textbook and gets down to business. I'm used to the way he acts during our lessons now, teacherish and businesslike, and I'm getting to like his serious approach.

"One thing strange about speaking," Joey begins, "is that some words sound alike even though they mean different things."

"Yes?"

"'To lip' sounds the same as the flower 'tulip'." Joey fingerspells the word "tulip".

I purse my lips into "tulip".

"No, Cat. Read my lips." I stare at Joey's lovely soft lips and watch as he repeats the word. "Tulip. Tulip. Tulip."

"Tulip, tulip, tulip," I say, pursing my lips as if to kiss and copying his shape with mine.

"You've got it!"

"To lip-read tulip," I mouth, smiling at the silliness of it.

"Hey, that'd be a great new sign name for you! Tulip. You want to lip-read and you look like a tulip." Joey makes the sign for tulip, sending all memories of Myra's horrible sign floating away on a cloud of joy.

"How do I look like a tulip?" I ask happily.

"Tall and slim with red on top."

Joey touches my red hair, then with a flourish he hands me an imaginary tulip.

And it is the best moment of my entire life.

Chapter Eighteen

It's official. I'm going out with Joey.

We're careful not to publicize it (that'd be suicide with the deaf city war going on) but everyone suspects, and not one of the signer boys has dared ask me to the ball. Probably Bee told them what kind of answer to expect.

End-of-term activities have started now and there are tons of things going on. Apart from preparations for the ball, Bee's play starts tomorrow – the same day as the debate – so we're both total wrecks. Today's the regional cross-country finals and although my leg's healing nicely, they won't allow me to participate, so Myra had better win for the school! Letting the team down makes me feel awful, but I can't do anything about that.

I must concentrate on what I have to do.

Tomorrow I'll be putting my head on the block with "The deaf should fit in with the hearing world" and I need all my wits about me for that.

The one good thing, the most spectacular, exciting, wonderful thing, is that tonight is the Outsiders' trip to the fair and since my speech-reading grades have improved (thanks to Joey!), Apeman's letting me join it. So it's not only a victory for me but...

My first real date with Joey!

I want to dance, shout and fly across the school, but instead I make do with writing a letter to my mum. The strain of actually going out with someone is just too much for a former wallflower like me!

As it's the end of term, Bee and I are lucky to have got the last two armchairs in the corner of the senior common room. There's an end-of-term relaxed atmosphere, and kids are lazing about, watching cartoons (relieved not to have to concentrate on reading subtitles), talking to friends or reading magazines.

In my letter I very casually mention the trip tonight but I leave out the bit about Joey. No point getting Mum in a state about me growing up too fast! Since she's missed out on so much of my childhood, she tends to see me still as her little girl. I decorate my letter with tulips (my favourite flower!) because since learning that Mum never actually left me in the hospital, I do lots of little things to show her things are better between us.

Mum and I've talked a lot on the minicom lately about when I had meningitis. She thought I was too ill to be conscious of much then, and she's been really amazed at how much I was aware of. She told me it's been just as much a relief for her as for me to be able to talk about it at last. Apparently it practically killed her when she had to let me go to deaf city, but she had to do it because she felt it was the best thing for me. She was right.

I address the envelope and stick it down. Bee looks at me questioningly. "Did you tell your mum you're going on the trip tonight?"

"Yes."

"I don't know why you don't do what I suggested," she argues.

"You mean tell Joey that fairground rides make me throw up? I don't think so!"

"It might bring out Joey's protective instincts."

"But certainly not his romantic ones."

Sometimes I wonder if I'll ever get Bee to see things from my point of view. Lately we can't agree on anything. I look at her hair as it fans across her shoulders like melted toffee, and a wave of affection comes over me. I *must* get her to understand! "Bee, you know your favourite picture in *Alice in Wonderland* when you were little? The one of Alice looking through that tiny garden door."

"What about it?"

"Alice wants to go through that door to get to the garden on the other side."

"What's this got to do with a stupid trip?"

"Don't you see?" I sign. "Going outside is like going through Alice's door to another world."

"Yeah, right." Bee's apricot cheeks redden. "Speakers fight being deaf. But that's what they are. Deaf, deaf, *deaf*! That's what we all are! Why don't you accept it? You're *never* going to hear!"

I shrink back as if every word is a blow. "Don't you think I know that? Deep down I know I'm deaf every second of my life. It's there when I eat, when I think, when I breathe..."

"That's the trouble with you. You can remember

140

being a hearie. To you deafness is a *giant weight* hanging over you."

"I just don't see why I can't be part of the hearing world."

Furious tears glitter in Bee's eyes. "You can't be part of the hearing world! You're nothing but a deaf and dumb dreamer!"

Ouch.

"They'll never accept us outside," Bee goes on, heedless of my pain. "They treat us like second-class citizens." Bee does a cruelly accurate imitation of a do-gooder. "Oh, isn't it nice to help those poor deaf retards! I just *love* the cute way they sign!"

"Don't!"

"Oh, go on the outside! I don't give a" – Bee makes a rude sign – "*what* you do!"

"You don't mean that, Bee."

"I do." She jumps up. "I'm sick and tired of defending you. You've even made me feel bad with my friends. I practically lost Jack..."

I swallow. "Bee! Why didn't you tell me?"

"Because you've been too busy with your stupid speech lessons and your yapping speaker boyfriend!"

"But if only—"

Bee holds up her hand to stop me. "Oh, I don't care any more. Go outside if you want to!"

"Bee—"

"You're just as much a dreamer as stupid Alice in Wonderland!" With that she runs out in floods of tears.

So that's how my best friend feels!

She wants me to choose between deaf city and outside, between her and Joey. But can't I be loyal to both? Why should I give up the chance of going out with Joey? Why should I give up trying to speak?

I spend the rest of the day lying alone on my bed, crying or staring at the ceiling, trying to decide what to do. But there's no answer there.

As the afternoon wears on, I do what I always do when I'm nervous, which is pace the room, twisting bits of hair round my fingers. It turns my mop into a huge mass of long curls, instead of the usual bush, and when I catch sight of myself in the mirror, I can't help thinking it's a shame no one will see it looking so pretty. Hanging on the wardrobe are my blue jumper and jeans, which I'm wearing tonight because Joey said he loved blue. Holding the jumper against my face, I'm surprised at how it makes my eyes greener and my hair redder than ever.

Red, like a tulip. "Tulip, tulip, to lip-read..." I say to the mirror, watching my mouth shape the words. To lip-read. I want to lip-read. I *want* to lip-read.

I will go on the trip!

But later, when I make my way to where a knot of speakers wait for the bus, talking together, I couldn't feel more nervous. Maybe Bee was right. Maybe I shouldn't be here.

With a thumping heart, I search for Joey, but he's not there.

He's not there! He's not there!

If only I could slip away into the shadows unnoticed, but Laurie Dean sees me and a scowl crosses her perfect face. She turns and mouths something to her friend, and together they start talking and laughing at me.

I'll never fit in here! Sick and defeated, I turn to walk away.

Then someone grabs my arm.

Chapter Nineteen

It's Joey.

Joey in jeans and a denim jacket (and denim never looked so good on anyone). "Hi, Cat," he says, using voice and sign. "Apeman's just giving his speech."

Apeman's standing on the steps of the bus, but although the lighted windows of deaf city illuminate his face, I can only catch a word here and there because he isn't using any sign.

"Keep ... group ... meet..."

Everyone but me understands. I must've been mad to want to do this! Maybe Bee was right.

But my enemy is not the people outside, it's Laurie Dean herself, gorgeous in a pink angora sweater and ice-pink trousers. She walks up to

Joey, her glossy lips moving. *She* has a weapon much more powerful than any axe.

Her voice.

Laughing and talking, the crowd surges forward to board the bus and Joey motions me to follow while he stops to speak with Apeman. So with Laurie's twitching behind right in my face, I slowly climb the steps.

Inside the narrow aisle of the bus, someone gives me a shove. It's my old enemy, Sammy Jackson. "Well, what d'you know? We have a token signer," he sneers.

"Watch it, Sammy," warns Joey, who's right behind him.

Sammy shrugs and, pointedly using sign, adds, "Nice to know we're becoming *integrated*."

Plonking myself into a seat, I feel as if all the oxygen has been sucked out from my body, leaving me like a burst balloon.

Apeman is up front, giving last-minute instructions in voice and sign. Thank you, Joey, for reminding him to stick with total communication! "Keep these seats on the return trip," Apeman says. "Make a note of who you're sitting next to."

I don't need to be told that!

Laurie Dean has managed to position herself across the aisle from Joey and she leans over and monopolizes him, shaking her blonde curls and talking to him the entire journey. I just turn and stare out of the window to show I don't care. But I watch every one of her sneaky, flirty expressions in the reflection in the window, and I'm convinced from the back of Joey's head that he's enjoying them.

OK, Laurie Dean. You're not the only one who can play at that game.

As soon as the bus stops in the car park, I jump up and push Joey ahead of me down the aisle while my rival is still searching for something in the luggage rack. And Joey and I are alone together, out in the fresh air, before you can say Laurie Dean.

"Come on, Joey," I say, stroking his arm. "This is our night."

There's a sparkle in Joey's eye when he replies, "Why, Cat! I'm beginning to see a new side of you."

And I'm beginning to see a new side of Joey...

In no time at all we've knocked down plastic ducks, ridden the carousel, thrown hoops and shared three hot dogs. Now we're in the games

146

arcade, and as I watch Joey play pinball, I feel just like any other girl having fun on a Friday night. Maybe I'm not so different from hearing girls after all! The pinball machine flashes a million lights as Joey's ball hits another post.

"Wow! You're good, Joey!" He's just hit jackpot for the third time in a row.

By now, Joey's expertise has attracted a crowd of onlookers. One thousand, five thousand, the ball zigzags, slamming against the posts. I hold onto the machine, thrilled with the excitement of the vibrations as the ball bounces against the numbers...

Jackpot!

Joey waves his fists victoriously and a guy in a leather jacket shouts something at him. Joey points to his hearing aid and shakes his head. "I'm deaf," he explains, but the guy persists in talking. Poor Joey has to concentrate hard on his lips, and finally he says something in reply which results in a lot of thumping and congratulating.

"You were terrific, Joey," I tell him proudly as we move away.

"I know," he jokes and we both laugh.

This is me. Me, walking with Joey Estrada. He motions me to a candyfloss booth and when his

147

hand touches mine, electricity shoots up my arm.

"Want some candyfloss?"

"Love some."

"You spoke!" Joey says approvingly, then he turns and speaks naturally and easily to the lady serving candyfloss. "Two, please."

"OK." The candyfloss lady mouths her answer exaggeratedly, then she takes two sticks and dips them into the swirling pink dust until two pink sticky clouds appear. And maybe it's because we are deaf, or maybe it's because we look happy together, but she makes them extra big for us.

"Are you sure this is edible?" I giggle, tugging at the pink fluff with my teeth.

"Of course it is. Pink dye number two strengthens the vocal chords."

I laugh again. "Hey, Joey, I want to ask you something. What did that man at the pinball machine say?"

"He said I was like the kid in the sixties rock musical *Tommy*. You know, the deaf, dumb and blind kid called the Pinball Wizard."

I feel my face grow hot with embarrassed anger. "Just because we're deaf, hearies think we're *dumb* too!"

148

Joey shrugs. "Don't get so upset. He meant it as a compliment. Anyway, I *am* a pinball wizard. As the song says, I've got no distractions." Joey gives a wicked smile and puts his arm round my shoulders. "Well, maybe just *one*..." And suddenly I feel as light as the candyfloss in my hand as all my anger dissolves into soft, sweet air.

Together we stroll away from the fair and look up at the stars for a long time.

"It's so beautiful here," signs Joey after a while. "We must come again in the summer."

"Yes," I say, so happy that he's making future plans, I use my voice without embarrassment.

There is a long eye-holding moment when neither of us can say a word, then Rob Walker (who tonight *is* wearing his hearing aid!) taps us from behind. He's with his girlfriend, Beth.

"We've just had our fortunes told by Madam Zarcati," Rob tells us.

"You should try her," adds Beth and she points to a red curtain with a yellow sign in the shape of an eye which says: MADAM ZARCATI – SHE TELLS ALL.

Joey grins. "Want to risk Madam Zarcati telling us all?"

"Why not."

Madam Zarcati's booth is painted with all kinds of weird symbols of the occult, but behind the red curtain is an ordinary old beach chair with a wooden sign in the shape of a hand pointing to another curtain, which reads: THIS WAY. TWO POUNDS.

I have to stifle a laugh as Joey lifts up the curtain. He turns to me with one raised eyebrow. "She says to come in."

Inside the dim, curtained area stuck with peeling suns and moons, Madam Zarcati is seated at a little circular table. She is trying to look mysterious and magical but to me she looks more like she just got out of the bath, with her flowing satin robe and fancy shower-cap thing on her head. Another wave of laughter threatens but fizzles out quickly at the sight of Madam Zarcati's haughty face. I've never seen so much make-up on an old person. She stubs out a cigarette with black painted fingernails and shoves the smouldering ashtray out of sight under the table.

"Four pounds."

She doesn't waste any time!

We pay, and Madam Zarcati cuts a pack of tarot cards. She shuffles in a bored fashion, muttering unintelligibly. Then she flips the cards onto the table and spreads them in rows, moving her ringed fingers expertly. After a lot of swaying and muttering, she looks at me. "You..."

I squeeze Joey's arm and he interprets.

"She's ... she's telling you that ... you're in trouble," he relays to me.

"Trouble! What kind of trouble?"

"Dunno. She's saying that you are in danger."

Under my soft blue jumper my heart palpitates.

Danger?

Suddenly I have to get out. The stupid peeling moons, Madam Zarcati and the claustrophobic booth are suffocating me, and I'm scared.

"Come on, Joey. It's time to get back to the bus."

Madam Zarcati's false eyelashes flip up in surprise as we make our exit. She may not read sign language, but she gets the message.

"Are you OK?" asks Joey as, outside, I gulp mouthfuls of fresh air.

"W-what danger did she mean, Joey? The debate is tomorrow. Did she see that in the cards?"

Joey shakes his head. "Madam Zarcati is a fake. The only danger is in believing her."

"I hope you're right."

"It's probably just guesswork. You're nervous about tomorrow and she picked up your vibes." Joey smiles reassuringly. "Don't worry, Cat..." Gently, very softly, he strokes my cheek, and then he leans towards my face and softly touches my lips with his.

It's the best first kiss any girl, deaf or hearing, ever had!

I kiss him back and then we just hold each other. We hold and hold each other, and it's like we were made to be that way.

I don't know how long we stay like that but suddenly Joey pulls away and looks at his watch. "Oh no!" he says. "You were right about what you said at Madam Zarcati's. We're going to miss the bus!" He pulls my arm. "Come on!"

Together we start to run, through the fair, and out into the car park, and we don't sign another word till we reach the deaf city bus.

It's impossible to sign when you're holding hands.

Chapter Twenty

Deaf city is in total darkness when we get back.

"Now remember not everyone's *completely* deaf around here." To make his point, Apeman signs without using his voice. "So make your way quietly to your dorms. See you all at the debate tomorrow." He gives me the thumbs up. "Good luck, Cat." It's his way of saying he's pleased with me.

"Thank you, sir."

Joey gives me a tender smile. "I'll be rooting for you, Tulip."

"Thanks, Joey. And thank you for a wonderful time."

Joey's answer to that is a goodnight kiss.

I have never felt so happy.

But, euphoric as I am, making my way through

dark, empty corridors searching for light switches starts to unnerve me. The others have gone in different directions to their own dorms, but I have to go through a deserted classroom block to get to mine. The corridors stretch endlessly, and the classrooms look eerie in the moonlight.

Suddenly a shadow flickers across a wall.

Oh my God!

Another shadow. Then another.

Someone is following me!

I steal a look behind me, but although I can't see anyone, I can *feel* them. Maybe it's true what they say about deaf people having an extra sense, because I *know* I'm being followed...

I quicken my pace.

All at once, three shadowy figures are silhouetted in the dim light of the corridor behind me, and one of them has long spindly legs and an insect-small body ... *Myra!*

Run!

Down the halls I run. I'm a good runner, but my newly healed leg slows me down. Faster, faster ... round a corner, down another hall ... run, run, run.

Stairs ... one two. One. Two. My shin throbs. *Jump, Cat, jump. Down, down, down...* Stairs. Me.

Stairs ... me. Over and over, tumbling down to the bottom.

Hands grab my arms, my legs, my hair, and I'm dragged, kicking and screaming, down the corridor. *Let me go! Let me goooo...*

We reach a cupboard and someone knees me so viciously in the back, I lurch forward into the dark, bleach-smelling interior and land painfully on a bucket.

Suddenly the dark is shattered by blinding light, and a naked bulb sways drunkenly overhead. Shadows zigzag and shimmering spots dance in front of me to settle into the faces of Myra, Jude and Sherry.

Jude plants her bully body in front of me; Sherry's eyes blaze; but Myra is the scariest, looming over me like a great tarantula, curving her hand and waggling her fingers in it like a chattering tongue.

"That's not my sign name! My sign name is *Cat*!"

"Not any more ... speaker?" She kicks me to add emphasis. "Speaker?" Myra's mouth works, pretending to speak. "Stupid speaker! Think you can win, don't you!"

155

I won't let her see how scared I am. I won't. "What d'you want, Myra?"

Myra kicks me. "Stop seeing Joey Estrada!"

"No!"

Myra's eyes are cold slits of steel. "You will stop seeing your stupid speaker boyfriend!" She kicks me the hardest yet, right in my side, and it hurts, hurts, *hurts*...

"You *will* stop seeing him. Laurie Dean will see to that. She's Estrada's *real* girlfriend. Your speaker is a spy, only sucking up to you because he wants inside information on the debate."

"That's not true!" Fear and rage pound in my head. It can't be true. Joey wouldn't do that to me! He wouldn't, would he? He *couldn't*! Not even if Laurie is the most beautiful, popular *speaker* in the world. It's me Joey wants. Surely it's just Myra's hatred that makes her say such a thing? Surely, surely, surely...

She's not going to see that I'm worried. So I fight back, ramming home my point with force by using voice as well as sign. "What's your problem, Myra? Did you lose the race today?"

Myra's face turns white, her nasty secret exposed.

"So you lost the cup for deaf city! You thought you'd got rid of me, and then you went and *lost the cup...*"

With terrific force, Myra steps on my arm and holds it down until the pain is excruciating. "I think" – she makes the yapping sign – "she needs to have her waggling tongue ripped out." Grabbing a handful of hair, Myra yanks my head back while the other two hold me down. Then Myra forces open my jaw and tries to grab my tongue with her horrible bony fingers.

Ugh! I want to vomit. I retch. Then the ghastliness of it gives me animal strength and, with all the power I have left in my body, I clamp my teeth onto Myra's fingers.

"Aaaaaagh!"

Nails. Fists. Feet. Mine. Theirs. They punch. I hit. Buckets, mops and brooms crash around us. The noise must be deafening.

Six elbows. Six knees. Six feet ... kicking, kicking, kicking. Pain, pain, pain...

When my enemies have finished with me, they leave me huddled on the floor, a limp doll, a spent ball of pain, and lock the door behind them.

* * *

It's hopeless.

Flashing the light on and off doesn't work. Screaming does no good. There's no one around and no one would hear me anyway.

I sob as uselessly as I sobbed at the age of five. But no one rescued me then, and no one will rescue me now.

At some point I drift into a tortured sleep.

In my dreams I'm abandoned at the fairground. The carousel, so bright and exciting before, has become a menacing ride hurtling towards some dark unnamed danger. As I'm propelled round faster and faster the horses' eyes flash and their open mouths gape in a blurred whirlwind of fear. I'm calling for Joey, but of course he cannot hear me. Suddenly I'm trapped in Madam Zarcati's tent, trying to sign my debate speech, but my hands are tangled up in her curtains. As I struggle, the curtains turn into a giant spider's web covered with peeling yellow moons. I wake up, arms flailing, legs kicking into a reality that's just as awful.

The debate will be cancelled.

That's what Myra wanted.

Bee's play will go ahead, and all the time I'll be locked in here, suffocating in this dark tomb. I've been here so long my eyes are beginning to get used to the pitch black and I can make out shapes in the darkness. On the back wall ahead of me is something purple. Wait a second, it's ... *sky*!

It's sky and it's getting lighter!

I switch on the light and there, behind the rows of scouring powder and cartons of sponges, is a tiny window. It's small and narrow but I must get through. Wincing with the pain of my bruised and battered body, I pull a ladder over to me. Then, grabbing a scrubbing brush, I climb up and smash the thick glass until it's nothing but small, thick chunks. My whole body is in agony from the brutal kicking, but I don't care. I don't care. Inch by painful inch I ease myself through the window to the outside.

Chapter Twenty-one

Deaf city is a ghost town. It's so early that the dewy mists are still on the grass. No one's up. No one sees this bent, limping, bedraggled figure hobbling across the deserted school grounds...

Me.

Back in the dorm, I stand under the shower for as long as I can take it, wincing as the jet of water hits my bruised body. The hot shower really brings out the colours. Any other time I'd wake up Bee to show her!

But not today. Maybe never again... In the last twenty-four hours I've lost my best ever friend, my fabulous (but false!) boyfriend and all belief in myself as an attractive person.

How could I ever have believed Joey really liked

160

me? Ever? Because if what Myra says is true, I never really had him in the first place. It was all an illusion.

Gingerly I pat myself dry. Then I pull on a big old T-shirt, hobble back to my room and crawl into bed. I want to sleep and sleep for ever, blot out the pain, blot out the hurting knowledge... Instead I set my vibrating alarm for twelve o'clock.

I may be beaten as a girl, but not as a speaker.

I will not miss the debate.

The debate.

On stage.

Brain fogged, body bruised, heart beat ... beat ... beating.

Waiting behind the curtains. Not red curtains with peeling moons but school stage curtains of thick grey.

I can't do this, I can't...

The stage door opens and Aggy bustles onto the stage.

"Right now, Cat, Jack, remember, just do your best. I'm going to introduce you now. Count to thirty and come out. Good luck to both of you." She gives us an encouraging smile and slips through the curtains to the front, and with that

161

all my nightmares come flooding back…

Deserted. Abandoned. Not in a hospital. But on a dark stage, shrouded with thick curtains holding nameless terrors in their secret folds.

I can't do it. I can't do it.

"Now!" signs Jack, grabbing my arm. "Come on."

"Nooo…"

"Come on!"

Oh my God. I escaped from that cupboard to be here. I *must* go on… I must. Catching my breath, I stumble through the opening in the curtains and step out to see rows and rows of faces. Watching me.

Aggy is out there, standing in front of a long table, and signing to the faces. "There will be no interruptions during the opening speeches. After the rebuttals the floor will have a chance to give opinions. And now I'd like to introduce our speaker for the motion 'The deaf should fit in with the hearing world'. Her name is Debbie Katz, but most of you know her as Cat."

Everything is a complete blank.

I can't remember a word of my speech. Unable to move, I stare blankly at the blur of faces. Bee is in the front row and Joey is in the next but one seat, sitting next to Laurie. *His girlfriend*. She always knew it. I know it now. Their faces look up at me intently. Expectantly.

What do they want from me?

Rigid, I stare back out at them, and there is a long-drawn-out stillness that seems to go on for ever and ever.

Then, without warning, a kid in the third row breaks the stillness. She raises her hand and waves at me.

"Hi, Cat! I'm Sandy."

Sandy!

The girl who wrote that letter to me! That heart-felt letter that came along with all those requests and confessions.

How can I let those people down?

How can I let down that girl, who's just like the young girl I once was?

Holding on to this knowledge, I raise my pain-fully bruised arms to swing into big gestures. And along with my signs, just as I practised, I use my voice to speak.

I speak of being different, yet feeling the same. Of the beauty of sign language, and the liberation of speaking. But most of all I speak of the right of every deaf person to *choose* how they communicate. My voice is bad, I don't know all the words, but my signs are strong.

"And so if we want deaf power we must stop fighting! War is not the answer. If we want the world to listen we must stop fighting *hearing* people, but most of all we must stop fighting *one another*."

I plonk myself down, spent. Relieved.

The worst part's over.

But Jack, his hair standing up like a halo in the spotlight, is fighting back. And he's fighting good. "OK, let's get this straight. We're deaf and we're not ashamed of acting deaf. We're proud of our own language. Signing is natural to us. *That's* our liberation, not speech! My opponent here is a traitor. She's like every other speaker, copping out." In the audience speakers are starting to shout out, but Jack continues. "Cat's scared to be her *true* deaf self."

Something in me bursts at that insult and words that have been bubbling inside me since I was five spew out in a torrent of feeling. "This *is* the true me! I was hearing and I remember the hearing

164

world. It's part of me just like the deaf world."

Jack signs furiously for me to be silent. "Wait for rebuttal time!"

"Don't try to shut me up! This is right for me! Only *me*. Not you, not him, not her" – I point to the audience – "but *me*! It was cowardly *not* to be the real me! And I won't be a coward any more. Because I've had enough of pretending!"

Aggy breaks in. "I must remind you of the rules of the debate, Cat. No interruptions."

My heart thuds like a torturer's blows as I allow Jack to finish his indictment of me. "As you can see, my opponent has betrayed her own kind!" And he sits down, triumphant amidst cheers of approval.

There's nothing left to lose.

Everyone hates me. Hates me, uses me. Spies on me.

Taking a wad of questionnaires from the pile in front of me, I hold them up in the air. "OK, so I want to be able to operate in the hearing world! In these responses are plenty like me! Suffering in silence – secretly needing to share their pain with someone. You all have your own stories. You told them to me here, now share them with us!"

For a long, long moment there is stillness.

Then slowly but surely an arm in the front row goes up. A tanned arm, ending with a strong hand. "I'm afraid of people outside laughing at my robot voice," the hand says as the voice mirrors the words. Then proudly Joey tells the whole world the words that feel as if they've been lifted from my very heart. "Cat's courage in learning to speak has helped me face my fear."

I flash Joey a thank you smile that says it all. My love, my pride and my eternal gratefulness to him. Joey was with me all the time. How could I ever, *ever* have doubted it?

Bee looks at Joey and gives a nod of complicity. Somehow the barriers are down and for the first time Bee and Joey, a signer and a speaker, are united. Bee puts up her hand. "*I'm* afraid of people laughing at my signing," she admits. Then she stands up and faces the audience. "I'm a coward, but that's one thing Cat is not. She's brave, very brave, and I'm *proud*…" Bee looks like she's about to burst into tears and plonks herself back down in her seat to be comforted by Megan.

Bee, my best, best friend, for once your dramatics are right on target! "Thanks, Bee…" I know what it took to make that admission.

Gradually other hands go up. It's as if Joey and Bee have pushed the button on a time bomb and it's about to explode. All over the hall kids sign, shout and fingerspell, allowing their stories to come tumbling out. Stories of fear, frustration and anger. The stories of the deaf.

And nobody stops them.

"And so for the final summing-up." Aggy looks at me. "The speaker for the motion … Cat?"

My summing-up is brief. "I just hope deaf city can remain united as we are now because that's where our power lies."

The whole room bursts into frenzied applause.

Aggy's face is proud. "Well done, Cat. And Jack?"

Jack looks at me and smiles, and as he raises his fist in the deaf power salute, I raise my arm to make it with him.

The two of us stand there, our fists held high while the whole of deaf city cheer, clap and twist their hands in a moving sea of silent applause. The applause of the deaf. Then the sea of hands moves in one accord to make the deaf power salute.

I don't need to know who won the debate.

I don't need to hear the noise of clapping. As the air vibrates with the strength of this single united sign, I know.

It's the best sound I have ever felt.

LOVE AND OTHER FOUR-LETTER WORDS
Carolyn Mackler

Sammie Davis never expected sweet sixteen to be perfect. But then she didn't expect her parents to separate either, or to have to leave her cosy life in suburbia for a tiny apartment in New York City. She begins a hot and humid summer struggling with feelings of resentment, anger … and lust for the Johnny Depp look-alike in her apartment block. As the vacation rolls on, she makes friends and breaks friends, finds new depths to the word *love*, and comes to understand that with it come other four-letter words. Like *hate*; *loss*; *gain*. But most important of all, *grow*.

"I love Carolyn Mackler and welcome her lively debut novel! *Love and Other Four-Letter Words* will grab the reader from the first page." *Judy Blume*

"Carolyn Mackler is a wonderful new talent." *Paula Danziger*

FISH FEET
Veronica Bennett

Erik Shaw loves dancing and wants to audition for the Royal Ballet School. But that means making some tough decisions – such as giving up the Falcons football team and letting down old friends. Then there's Ruth, a fellow ballet dancer to whom Erik is becoming increasingly attracted. Can their relationship survive the rigours of practice and competition? And has Erik got the strength of will as well as the talent to achieve his goal?

PLANET JANET

Dyan Sheldon

Friday 22 December
I don't want to end up shallow and superficial like
so many other people (e.g. my family). I'm going to
be intense, serious, and spend a lot of time nurtur-
ing my soul. I'm also going to dress mainly in black.

Meet Janet. She's determined to explore Life's True
Essence, despite the countless hurdles in her way
(i.e. her mother the Mad Cow, a tragically lost
mobile, the trials of Romantic Love etc.). But while
she splashes around the Deep End of the Pool of
Life, could Janet be missing what's happening on
dry land?